The Bookkeeper

Amorous Occupations

Cheryl Barton

Published by:
Barton Book Publishing

Barton Book Publishing
P.O. Box 962
Reisterstown, Maryland 21136
www.crbarton.com

Ordering Information:
Quantity sales. Special discounts are available on quantity purchases by corporations, associations, and others. For details, contact the publisher at the address above.

Orders by U.S. trade bookstores and wholesalers.
Please contact prez@crbarton.com

ISBN: 0615881068
ISBN-13: 978-0615881065

Prologue

Karen Jacobs walked into her office to get information on her latest assignment. She'd just returned from a much-needed vacation and was eager to get back to work. She had been working for the FBI for seven years and she was about to get her first undercover assignment.

"Welcome back Ms. Jacobs," one of the office assistants said as she passed by.

"Thanks Tanya. I'm happy to be back."

"Did you have a nice vacation?"

She'd had a blast on vacation. She was an adventurist, so she had done everything from sky diving, rock climbing, deep sea diving and she loved every minute of it.

"I had a great time. I was actually supposed to have another week off, but duty calls."

"Well it's good to see you back. Mr. Jackson is in and he's waiting for you. You can go right in."

"Thanks Tanya."

Karen walked into her boss's office where he and two other agents were waiting to brief her on the assignment.

"Karen, good to have you back," Mr. Jackson said.

"Thanks. It's great to be back."

"Why don't you take a seat and we'll brief you on what we have."

Taking her seat, she opened up the folder that had been placed in front of her. Shock was the first thing that came to mind when she opened it and saw the face of Thomas Atwater. He was the owner of a major financial investment firm in the Raleigh, North Carolina area. He was also the man she'd walked away from ten years earlier because he had chosen work over his life with her.

Being a workaholic herself, she now understood his commitment to his work and now knew that she had been naïve and selfish back then. She had been a woman in love and he was a man on the rise in the business world who didn't have time for her. She had issued him an ultimatum and lost. She looked up from the folder into the faces of the men around the room. They knew everything about her and knew her connection to the man in the picture. It was clear to her that the reason she was chosen for this undercover assignment was because of the man in the photo, a lover from her past.

"What's this?" she asked, with great surprise.

She watched as everyone around the table looked to each other, but avoided eye contact with her until Mr. Jackson finally spoke up.

"This, Karen, is your assignment."

She looked from one man to the other wondering if this were some type of joke. There was no way they were asking her to do an undercover operation on a man who knew everything about her, including the most intimate things.

"You're not serious, are you?" she inquired searching their faces.

"Karen, we are very serious about this case. We've received some very reliable information that there are some unsavory financial dealings going on at Atwater Industries. It appears that Mr. Atwater has been involved in some illegal dealings and we need you to get in and check things out. We're setting you up as a temporary bookkeeper at his firm. The last Mr. Atwater knew about you, you were an accountant, so this should work out well with getting you in the door. He has no idea what you've been doing since he last saw you, so your identity as an agent is secure. His current bookkeeper is about to go out on maternity leave and this is the perfect opportunity to get you in under the radar."

To say she was shocked would be an understatement and she had no doubt they could see the reservation on her face. For starters, she knew Thomas and knew he wouldn't be dealing in anything illegal and she knew that with this scheme, they were reaching. Their plan sounded simple and though it may seem easy to them, she had a feeling it would not get past Thomas at all. He was too smart to think that after all of this time, she was willing to be a bookkeeper for him and it didn't matter what her background was or where she had been for the past ten years. Would he really believe that she hadn't made any strides beyond working with numbers? With the history they had, she couldn't imagine justifying getting a job at his firm. They hadn't ended things on the best of terms. To her, this was about to be a losing situation.

"He won't fall for this. He knows me and stepping in as a bookkeeper after ten years wouldn't be the me he would remember," she said.

"We know he wouldn't fall for the fact that you just happened to be coming in for a temporary position as a bookkeeper knowing that at that time when you last spoke, you were an accountant for a major firm. He wouldn't understand why you haven't progressed much further in your career. We're setting up a background for you that includes working in finance for a major corporation in Seattle and that you're coming back to the Raleigh area because you were tired of living on the west coast. You never did sell your parents' home after your mother passed away, so it was easy making a transition for you to be back in the area, moving back into the house that meant so much to you."

She shook her head, letting them know that she didn't think that all of this was going to be possible. What she didn't want to say was that she was hesitant with being deceitful with Thomas. They may have a rocky past, but she wasn't comfortable digging into his business, looking for information to destroy him. Could she really do it?

"You really believe he'll fall for that? So, what am I supposed to do, just walk into the front door of his company and apply for a job as a bookkeeper? Even with my history in accounting, I can't see just casually strolling in there to a man I walked away from years ago and asking for a job."

Karen couldn't picture anything along the lines of this going as smooth as they want her to believe. She was having a hard time wrapping her head around the fact that Thomas could be doing anything illegal or that he would easily accept her back into his space and doing so with her asking for a job.

Glancing down at the picture again, memories of Thomas flooded her mind. Her boss was talking about work, finance and illegal dealings and all she could think about was Thomas' kisses, caresses and the way he made love to her that often brought tears to her eyes he made her feel so good. This was a man she loved more than anything. She knew him and knew deep down, he wasn't doing anything illegal and she didn't care what the file said.

"We know, again from a very reliable source,

where Mr. Atwater will be having lunch Monday afternoon. We want you to casually stroll into the restaurant, not his company and happen upon him. You'll strike up a conversation as if you've forgiven him for the way things ended between you two. His lunch date will conveniently not show up and you'll sit down to join him until his guest arrives, like I stated, who won't actually show up. Try to start a conversation about what he's up to these days and push for it to lead in the direction of him telling you about his bookkeeper leaving his company to have a baby soon, leaving him in a pinch to find a replacement. This is what you've been trained to do and I have faith you can pull this off without a problem."

Karen started to see it playing out in her head and realized it just might work. Her director was right, she was trained for this. She had never doubted herself as an agent before and she wasn't going to start now. She was ready for this as long as she could keep images of her and Thomas between the sheets out of her mind. The man had a body like a well-trained athlete and she loved feeling his hardness against and inside of her. Thinking of him caused her body to tingle as she remembered what it felt like to be with him. She didn't doubt her work, but she was beginning to doubt her ability to be around Thomas and focus only on work.

"Now, Karen, the current bookkeeper is one of our sources. She claims that there are some tricky things going on with the money. There are lots of meetings behind closed doors and one day, she was looking at the books and realized she had never seen one of them before. It contained information about major deposits into an account she wasn't familiar with. She then discovered she had been looking at the wrong book and not the one she should have been looking at. She went out to lunch and when she returned, that wrong book had been mysteriously replaced with the correct book. Someone had switched them while she was out. She asked Mr. Atwater about it and he brushed it off as if he didn't know what she was talking about. He quickly changed the conversation and went about his day. She mentioned what she saw to her best friend's husband who is a police detective and from there, the information was passed on to us. Our initial investigation led us to several off-shore bank accounts in Mr. Atwater's name that contained funds that amount to much more than his company could make in a year's time."

Karen started to understand better now. They wanted her to find out what kind of on the side business Thomas was involved in and if it were anything illegal.

"I'm picturing how to play this out now," she said, feeling more confident.

Her boss smiled.

"I knew you would. You are our brightest agent and if anyone could pull this off, it's you. When he mentions the pregnant bookkeeper, lead in with the fact that you're back in the area and you had not yet taken on any new jobs as an accountant. Since the past is water under the bridge, you could help each other out by having you fill in for the bookkeeper until she returns. That way, you can make a little money while getting acclimated back to the area."

Karen reassured them she was on top of it and would to take the file back to her office and prepare for her move back to the Raleigh area where she'll work closely with the branch of the FBI located in that area.

After the briefing, she headed to her office where she closed the door behind her and opened the folder again studying its contents. She stared into the face of the one man she was never able to forget. He was the man who could play her body like a sweet guitar, picking every string that turned her into putty in his hands. She closed her eyes and remembered the many nights of passion they shared, knowing she had never met a man since who made her feel the way he had.

She looked down into the face of the most handsome man she'd ever laid eyes on and wondered if she were going to be able to resist him long enough to get her job done. She hoped so because everyone at the office would be counting on her. She could no longer be the Karen who was still madly in love with Thomas Atwater. She now had to be Karen Jacobs, the FBI agent who would find out about the illegal dealings and if she had to, she would make sure he was prosecuted to the fullest extent of the law.

Karen closed the file and walked to the window to look out. She knew she would do her job, but at the same time, she couldn't wrap her mind around the fact that the Thomas she knew would be involved in anything criminal. Either way, she would get to the truth and put her game face on to prepare.

1

The men had been sitting in the back of the moving van finishing up the last of eight hands of spades. They weren't really moving men, but agents posing as moving men on their latest case. The FBI had to make it look like Karen was actually moving back into town and into her parents' old home where she lived as a child.

Neighbors were always watching through windows, something Karen remembered growing up and she was sure that hadn't changed since she last lived there with her family. The plan had been put in place to stage the scene of a major move for her back to town by backing a truck up to the garage as if they would be moving lots of items out of it. They made sure to back it up far enough into the garage so that anyone passing by could not see that they weren't moving much, but a few small items and some luggage.

Karen's car was packed with other incidentals to add more reality to the scene. After a few hours, the men prepared to head out while Karen got settled in. She wasn't sure how many of the neighbors were in the area when she last lived in town. The only neighbor she knew still lived there was her next-door neighbor, Mr. Otis, because he had taken good care of the house while she was gone. He had dealt with the renters the first few years that she'd decided to rent the house and he agreed to continue looking after the place when she no longer wanted anyone living in it until she decided what to do with it. Karen walked through the house, letting her mind take her down memory lane when he appeared at the front door.

"Mr. Otis, it's so good to see you," she said as she opened the door to let him in.

"Ms. Karen, it's nice to have you back in the neighborhood. Are you getting settled in?"

"Yes I am. Can I get you some coffee or anything else to drink?" she asked.

"No thank you. I wanted to come by to say hello and to bring you your spare keys. I had the cleaners come by to get the dust off of everything when you called to say you'd be moving back in. Let me know if I can do anything else to help you. My wife and I are heading out for dinner and a movie so I won't take up a lot of your time. It really is good to see you in this house again."

"Thank you, Mr. Otis. It actually feels great to be back. I've been gone too long."

"Well, perhaps after you are all settled, you'll

join my wife and I for dinner one evening."

"That would be nice. I will let you know. Enjoy your dinner and movie and thanks for looking after everything," she said as she escorted him back out the door.

As he left, Karen realized it really did feel good to be back in Raleigh. She hadn't seen Thomas since her breakup with him many years ago, in this very room. Being back in the house brought back the memories of that last day they'd spent together in this very house. They had first spent a wonderful evening making love at his place when he mentioned moving to another state for yet another business opportunity. Karen had been so angry, she made him bring her back home and that's when the fight started.

"What do you mean it's you or my business? Do you hear how ridiculous you sound Karen?"

"Ridiculous, Thomas? Is that what you said? I love you. Is that ridiculous? I'm willing to sacrifice everything to be with you. Can you say the same thing?" she said enraged.

"Karen, you are asking me to sacrifice seven years of college and two more years of building my career to finally having the type of company that I want. I worked the last few years learning from one of the top companies in the North Carolina area and the purpose was so that I could one day start my own financial firm. Now that I'm doing that, you're trying to tell me that I have to

choose between my business and you? Why can't I have both? You can't see the benefit that having this company will be to any kind of life we plan to have?"

"Thomas, you promised me! You promised me that work would not completely take over you. I've waited all these years for you to first finish school, then do an internship, then spend fifteen hour a day work days learning how to build your own business and now that you have it, you spend even more time building this one. How many years will this take? I want marriage, I want children and I want a life with the man I love without having to compete with his company. I know you have dreams and I have them too. Do you think I want to work as a bookkeeper for the rest of my life? I don't, but I want you and children more than I want advancement in my career right now. My dad is gone, my mom has failing health and there are things more important in life than career and money," she pleaded.

"Is that what you think of me? That I'm placing career and money before you? I'm doing all of this for you; for us!"

Karen's frustration was on a new level now. Talking to Thomas was like talking to a wall. He never budged when he had his mind set on something.

"So, when Thomas? When are we getting married? Do you feel like I'm pressuring you? Am

I the only one who wants to get married? Did I waste all of these years waiting on you to obtain your golden goose only to realize you still aren't as successful as you'd like to be? Are you ever going to be ready to settle down? You spend every waking hour at your company and it's just getting off the ground. It will take years to get it where you want it to be. In the meantime, where does that leave me? I never see you much now and we never spend any time together anymore unless it's a quickie for sex, which you have no problem finding time to do."

"Don't do that Karen. Don't belittle the intimacy we share. I love you and you mean more to me than anything or anyone else in my life. Why can't you see that I'm doing all of this for us?"

They were engaged in a shouting match that Karen realized wasn't going anywhere. She had spent the better part of the last few years waiting on him to be ready, ready to make her his wife and ready to give her the babies she so desperately wanted. She thought she knew him and that they wanted the same things.

"Thomas, I'm not asking you to give up your dreams. I'm asking you for once to make me as much of a priority as your drive to have a successful company. Tonight, right after sex I might add, you tell me that you're moving out of state to take over a company that will be the beginning of fulfilling your dream of growing your

own firm."

"I asked you to come with me. I'm not trying to leave you behind, I want you with me," Thomas said.

"Thomas our life is here. What will I do with my mother? I can't just leave her here alone especially now when she really needs me."

"I need you too, Karen. Doesn't that matter? I would never ask you to leave your mother. There is room in our lives for your mother wherever we are and you know that."

"You don't have to do this to achieve your dreams. You are doing fine here. I know according to you, this is an opportunity of a life time, but there will be other opportunities and plenty of them I'm sure will occur right here in Raleigh. So once again, I'm being asked to wait for your next achievement. Well you know what, I'm not waiting anymore. Decide right now Thomas, what's more important to you, your life here with me or your life in New York without me."

Thomas looked at her stunned that she would issue him an ultimatum.

"You can't be serious Karen," he said alarmed that she might be.

Karen was determined to win. She knew in her heart that he would choose her if he thought that the alternative was that he would lose her for good. When he didn't immediately respond and choose her, the silence was deafening. She could *see the struggle he was having trying to make a choice.*

Thomas knew that he should choose her, but he couldn't understand why he couldn't have both. She was asking him to give up on his dreams for marriage and babies. They had plenty of time to do that, but now was the time for him to build a life for them. He didn't understand why she couldn't see that.

"I love you," he said, almost pleading with her to feel the depth of his love for her in his words.

Karen stopped breathing. His declaration of love sounded like he was about to say, 'but'.

"You can't choose, can you? You really can't choose. It shouldn't be this hard. Well, let me make it easy for you. Get out!" she shouted.

Thomas looked at her stunned as he tried to calm her down. He'd never seen her this angry before.

"Karen, we need to talk about this some more. I know there is a way for us to have it all."

"Get out Thomas. Get out! Get out! GET OUT!," she shouted through the tears that started to fall. All the years they'd spent together and she was not a priority to him.

"You can't mean that, Karen."

"I never want to see you again," she cried, no longer able to hold back the tears.

Thomas knew there was no changing her mind when she turned away from him. He turned toward the door, opened it and left.

After the door closed, Karen fell to the floor and cried for all of the years she'd wasted waiting on him to figure out what was important in life. She cried for the wedding she wouldn't get to have and for the children she wouldn't be having with him because though he declared his love for her, his love didn't put her first. She'd spent years doing so much for others, including her family, that she wanted and needed to be first in his eyes. She was crushed to think that she wasn't. She really thought that he would choose her. How could she have been so wrong?

Karen remembered that night as if it had just happened. She, even now, could still remember feeling defeated, crushed and depleted. Now she was back in the same house, standing in the same room where they had last talked.

She'd kept up with his rise in the business world over the years. She knew that he had in fact left town a few weeks after their last encounter. After that night, she did everything she could to avoid running into him and she ignored his many phone calls pleading for her to change her mind. She leaned on her best friend Lacey back then to help hold her up and make it through. Nothing seemed to help her get over the loss of her relationship with him. She had hoped he wouldn't be able to live without her and she waited for him to show up and declare that he chose her; that he was sorry for second guessing his decision to not choose her, but in all of his messages, he was still convinced that she should come with him. She waited day after day for him to come to his senses, convinced that some time apart would do the trick. Then one day Lacey showed up at work where they both worked as bookkeepers and told her that she's heard Thomas had finally left town. She was devastated.

Karen had still been living with her mother at the time, so she didn't want to go home and cry. She instead rented a hotel room and cried for two days before finally picking herself up and going on with her life. Life had been dealing her a really bad hand and later that same year, her mother passed away and after that, she didn't think twice about packing up and moving far away from the town she just wanted to forget about. She had lost both of her parents and the love of her life to this town and she vowed never to return. She'd taken the money her parents had left her and her own savings, got her neighbor to agree to look after the property and she moved to the other side of the country.

Finding a job had been easy after one month of living in Seattle, Washington. She had landed a job with a major investment firm as an entry level accountant. It was there that she decided to take the exam to work for the FBI and passed the entrance exam with flying colors. Her career with them began with her working in their investigative unit doing research on cases. It was a major case investigating a large financial corporation and they needed someone good with numbers and money and she fit the bill. Once she moved up in the agency, she spent years working towards being a member of the undercover unit and when she moved up, she then moved to DC and never looked back.

Over the years, she'd dated, but nothing serious. Her job took up most, if not all of her time and she only had time for casual dates, nothing long term. Now she was back in the town that she vowed she'd never come back to. Being in Raleigh didn't provide her with as many happy memories as she'd like, but she had a job to do. She shook off thoughts of a life in her past and reached for the files that contained everything she needed to know about the case against Thomas. She headed to the kitchen for some food knowing she'd need a full stomach in order to deal with the fact that she was working on a case that could possibly land the only man she truly ever loved in jail.

2

Thomas was disappointed at the outcome of his date earlier in the evening. Lately, he'd been going through women as often as he changed his clothes. He knew the issue wasn't with the women because all of them were beautiful, successful and into him. He couldn't seem to connect to any of them beyond the bedroom.

He'd dated a lot of women over the past few years, but dating wasn't leading to the relationship he wanted to invest his time, energy and heart into. He hadn't had that since Karen Jacobs, the one woman who was able to capture his heart from the moment he'd met her back in his high school days. She may have left his life, but she'd never left his heart. He'd tried to find a replacement for that kind of love many times, but no one could hold a candle to what Karen was to him.

"Can I get you anything else before I leave?"

Thomas was startled by the sudden appearance

of his housekeeper, Sarah. He'd been so caught up on his thoughts of days in the past that he forgot that he wasn't alone.

"No, Sarah. I'm good."

"I wasn't expecting you home so early this evening. I take it your date didn't go as well as planned?"

Thomas looked at her with a face that showed that he had no doubt she knew him too well.

"You are correct."

Sarah came into the living room where he came in and sat when he first arrived.

"What happened this time or do I want to know?" she asked smiling. He knew she was making an attempt to lighten his mood.

"I don't know. I'm sure whatever it was, it was with me. Vivica is absolutely beautiful and we had a great time at dinner. She invited me back to her place and of course you and I won't talk about what that meant, but I declined and came home. I used a work excuse to hopefully let her know the issue wasn't with her, but with me. Believe me, when I saw her in that little black dress, I wanted to skip dinner and head straight to her hotel since she's only in town for this one night, but going from bed to bed is getting old."

"That's because you finally want more than that. These women you serial date are all lovely I'm sure, but when you think further on what a future would be like with them, they aren't enough or you're just being too picky. Which is it?"

"I think it's a little of both."

"I'm sure there is a woman out there that has everything you want and need and hopefully you're allowing yourself to be open to that."

Thomas nodded his head, not wanting to tell her that he'd let that woman slip through his fingers and he had lived in regret ever since. There was guilt over the fact that he didn't do more to convince Karen that she was the most important thing in his life and he had enough room in it for her and his dreams. They were supposed to dream big together.

After moving to New York after their breakup, he'd kept up with her for a little while, but once her mother had passed away and she moved to the west coast to Washington, he'd lost track of her. The intensity of their connection was a once in a lifetime occurrence and their love should have been enough. He hadn't found a love like that since her and the life of having it all in his business and personal life was lacking on the personal side.

"There is. Do you know that I had a lot of my life planned out, which I shouldn't have done because that only leads to a feeling of emptiness? By now, I was supposed to have a wife, a few kids and enjoying the fruits of my hard work and sacrifices over the years."

Thomas surprised himself at the somberness of his tone, but not having his mother or father around while he was growing up, he wanted to have a family and be that father he wished he'd had. He and Karen had talked about having children and he'd set out to make sure they would live a comfortable life so that by the time they had children, he wouldn't be the workaholic he knew he could be. That hadn't panned out and the last he'd heard, it hadn't panned out for Karen either. She hadn't gotten married or had any children. He thought a few times about reaching out to her best friend, Lacey, to try and get in contact with Karen. He'd been thinking about her over the years and lately, she'd invaded more than a few of his dreams.

"You are a great man, doing great things and every woman would be lucky to have a caring, loving and stable guy like you. Don't be so picky. I don't think every woman will have everything you want, but find what you can live with."

Thomas looked over at her knowing he was being too hard on himself.

"One woman had everything."

Sarah knew who he was referring to. They'd talked several times about the love of his life that he'd let get away and she knew that he wishes he could go back and change things between them.

"I know Thomas and so will another one. Would you like me to fix you anything before I leave?"

"Is there any of your lasagna left from yesterday?"

"Sure, I can heat it up for you."

"No, I can do that. I have some paperwork to look over and I'll heat it up myself in a little while. I wanted to be sure there was some left. Go ahead home and take tomorrow off. I'm going to be out all day in meetings and won't get back until very late."

"If you're sure, then I'll see you on Tuesday. I'm making my world-famous pot roast for you."

Thomas smiled. Sarah knew how to make any situation better. She'd been his housekeeper and chef since the day he'd moved back to North Carolina and she was hands down, the best cook. He loved southern cooking and she laid it on thick.

"You know how much I love your pot roast. I'm surprised I'm not a big, hefty executive with all of your good cooking. It's a good thing I work out every day or no woman would ever give me a second look," he laughed.

"Hmmp. I've seen how women look at you and heavy or thin or even beefy like you are now," she chuckled, "there will never be a shortage of them who will want to be the woman you choose. I look forward to the day when I can hear little feet running around here to greet me and beg for the cookies I you'll try and be hard and deny them. I'm just as excited about the possibility as you are. I'm going home and I want you to promise me you'll stop thinking about what you don't have and be happy for the life you have. I know it feels like something is missing, but it's not. You're just in the waiting room waiting for the rest of your life to find you and it will."

Thomas got up and gave Sarah a hug. She has always been more than just someone who keeps his life and house in order and he loved her like a mother.

"I promise," he said.

3

"Can you feel me, Karen?"

"Yes, Thomas, I feel everything."

Karen moaned and squirmed with every touch of Thomas' hands up and down her thighs, caressing her into submission with every stroke of his fingers' light touches on her skin. She felt on fire and more aware of him than she'd ever been before. His hands, though on her legs, felt as if they were moving all over her body at once. She was barely able to contain herself the moment one of his hands slid further up her legs and encountered the smooth softness of the entrance into her body which was already wet and waiting for him.

Thomas moved up to nuzzle her neck, licking and kissing a wet path from one side to the other and then blowing on the moist strip, causing her body to gyrate with anticipation. She had never wanted him more than she did right now.

"I need you," she practically begged.

"I need you too baby and I can't wait to be inside

of you, but first, I have another need; the need to taste your sweetness. It's all I've thought about all day," he muttered close to her ear, driving her wild. Karen felt her body's attempt to leap from the bed the moment his hot, moist tongue licked across her earlobe before darting in. As his tongue drove her wild with want and need for him, Thomas used that exact moment to slide a finger inside of her as wetness covered his finger, slipping from her. The slippery sound of his finger going in and out and the luscious feeling of his ministrations had her on the brink of a powerful orgasm.

"I can't hold it," she moaned out loud, now moving her hips and thrashing wildly on the bed.

Thomas increased the pressure of his finger while using his thumb to stroke her hardened nub.

"I don't want you holding back, but I do want to taste you as you come apart," he said quickly sliding down her body, spreading her legs wide to accommodate his body and replacing his finger with his tongue. Karen braced herself for the onslaught of the explosion she knew was about to occur, when the moment was interrupted by the sound of a phone ringing. The sound got louder and louder and before she knew it, she was startled awake.

Karen sat up straight, barely able to catch her breath as she looked around at her surroundings. She wasn't in bed with Thomas who was about to give her another one of those incredible orgasms.

She was alone, on the sofa where she'd drifted off to sleep. Becoming more aware of the fact that she had been having a salacious dream about Thomas, not the one from years ago, but the face of the one in the photos that she'd been studying of him now, hot, sexy and well-aged. Dream or no dream, she was more turned on than she'd been in a long time. She reached up and felt the sweat on her brow and the thin layer of the shirt she was wearing was not stuck to her chest. The area between her legs was pulsating as if she had actually been touched there, but it was a dream; it was only a dream.

More aware of the memory of her life with Thomas, she shook it off when realized the ringing of the phone was real and not a dream. She stood quickly to grab it from the table while trying to get her breathing in check. She grabbed it before the caller hung up and noticed it was a call from her best friend, Lacey Dawson.

"Kay," is what she heard when she answered. She and Lacey had been best friends since childhood and the only person in the world who called her Kay. She had called Lacey to let her know what was going on and she was the only friend who knew about her work as an undercover agent for the FBI. She didn't trust anyone else with that information and as far as others were concerned, she still worked in accounting.

"Lace! It's about time you returned my call."

"I know and I'm sorry I'm slow getting back to

you. I didn't recognize the number when you called and I didn't have time to listen to the message until today. I waited until Kevin left to take the boys to the baseball game before I called you back."

A little bit of jealousy seeped through Karen at the mention of Lacey's husband and their two sons whom Karen was godmother to. Lacey was living the life she had once longed for with a husband and children. Lacey's husband, Kevin, spoiled her rotten and the boys ages six and four were the light of her life.

"It's okay. How are my godsons? After this case is over, I plan to come for a visit. I need a big old Texas steak!"

"Girl, they are fine and growing like weeds. I'll tell them you called. So, let's chit chat later. Right now, I want to hear about this case you're on and what's it got to do with Thomas. Have you seen him yet? What kind of trouble is he in? I want to hear it all."

Karen chuckled at her Lacey's eagerness.

"Okay, well for starters if you call me, use this number. I had to leave the other phone in DC. I'm having a phone turned on in the house in a few days and I'll make sure you get that number too. As for Thomas, no I haven't seen him yet and it seems he's in a lot of trouble. It appears money is being embezzled from the employee's retirement fund and being transferred to an off-shore bank account in Thomas' name. He didn't do it I'm sure and I still have much more to read about what the FBI has discovered so far, but most of their leads have been dead ends. Thomas as a thief can't possibly be true and I don't believe any of this case that's being built up against him."

Karen knew that would get Lacey stirring.

"Wait, did you say he didn't do it?"

"That's exactly what I said. He didn't do it. He couldn't have."

"Kay, if you know that then what's with the assignment?"

"I didn't say they don't think he did it or that the finger isn't being pointed at him as the culprit. I'm saying I don't believe he did it. Come on Lacey, you know him just like I do and if nothing else stands out when it comes to Thomas, I know that he's honest and he wouldn't steal from anyone, especially those who work for him. I don't care how many years it's been since I've last spoken to him, I know he's worked hard to get where he is and wouldn't throw it all away to steal when he's smart enough to make plenty of money without having to resort to that. It's not in him and if you think about the Thomas we both know, though we hate him for what he did to me years ago, he's no thief."

She smiled when Lacey laughed.

"Okay, so we're still hating him? You have to let me know these things just in case I see him. I want to remember that I'm still giving him the cold shoulder."

Karen laughed.

"Okay, maybe we're not hating him as much as we did back then. Have you seen what he looks like lately? That man is even more fine than he was back then. No one can hate a man that good looking."

"I see your memory has kicked in. Thinking of those past hot, sexy nights you spent with him, are you?"

"Stop it Lacey. I have to keep my mind on this case and not on how hot and sexy Thomas is; I mean was."

"Oh, no chick. You had it right the first time. I've seen the tons of magazine covers with him on it and time has done him well."

"Yes, it has, but that doesn't overshadow the fact that I have a job to do."

"Right, but can't you get in a little time to do him too? I'm just saying," Lacey said.

Karen laughed again.

"Only you would go there. I can't do Thomas. That is water under the bridge that has since dried up. That's history."

"It doesn't have to be."

"Yes, Lacey it does."

"No, Karen it doesn't. Not if you don't want it to be."

"It does and I have to stay focused."

Lacey gave up.

"Okay, so how are you going to handle this.

What's the plan?"

Karen hadn't thought a lot about what she was planning to do. There was a lot more to discover about the case.

"Well, right now I'm trying to figure out what to do. I don't like being dishonest, even when it comes to Thomas. He hurt me years ago, yes, but even that hurt could never cloud my judgment and make me think he's some kind of crook now. I've looked over a lot of the information on the case and there's still lot's more to review. Unless I'm on the inside I don't think I'll be able to find out what's really going on. I just don't know how much I should tell Thomas."

"Wow, Kay. If you are going to do this, you can't tell him anything. Remember you took an oath and no matter what, you still have a job which you have to do even without compromising your position or letting Thomas know that he's being investigated. I know you want to help him, but in doing so, don't risk your job by letting him in on it. You can still do your job while looking into who the real thief is can't you?"

Karen thought about it for a minute.

"I guess I can. I just feel like I'm being dishonest. Actually, *I am* being dishonest, but I don't know how else to help him without first deceiving him. I don't want to hurt him Lace, even after all these years, I don't want to hurt him."

"You won't hurt him if you find out who really is

doing this. Once you do that, you can explain to him what's really going on and I'm sure he'll understand that you were only trying to help. You'll also please your boss by doing the job he assigned to you and instead of trying to find information to convict a man, you're trying to find out what really is going on at the company. I believe it's a win all around."

"I guess you're right. I was just about to dive into the rest of the files when you called. I'm a little nervous about seeing him again. I've kept track of him all of these years and I know he's very successful and I'm happy for him."

"I'm sure you also know that like you, he never married and doesn't have any children either."

Karen knew sooner or later the conversation would turn from work to a more personal one.

"Yes Lace, I know that. I knew that before I read it in the file. I guess he's been too busy building his empire. You know how important that has always been to him. When was the last time you've seen Thomas in person?"

"Let me think. I saw him once from a distance when I took the boys to Raleigh for a family reunion about two years ago. I saw him, but he didn't see me."

"I haven't seen him since that last day here at the house."

Karen opened up the folder and looked down at the recent pictures of him. He was still just as handsome as he was back when they dated. The biggest difference in his appearance was that he was now bald and it looked good on him. In one of the full body photos, she could see that he still maintained his incredible physique and as always, he looked scrumptious in a suit.

Another picture showed him sitting in a restaurant and something his guest said must have made him smile because he was smiling happily and it made her remember all of the times she sat across from that gorgeous smile. It melted her heart then, just as it was doing now through the picture.

"Kay, are you going to be able to deal with being around him again. I know it's been a lot of years and you didn't end on good terms?"

She wondered the same thing.

"I don't know, girl. I'm working my way up to it. I'll call you Monday evening to let you know how it goes on the first day."

"So, Monday is the day huh?"

"Yes. There is a plan in place for us to casually run into each other, so I have to get my game face together. I can't blow this by foaming at the mouth when I see him or stammering like a bumbling idiot, so I'm working it out. These pictures of him really take me back and he is still gorgeous. No man should look this good in or out of clothes."

Before she realized what she'd said, it was already out of her mouth.

"Your heart still loves him even if your mouth won't say the words and it's okay to feel that way.

I've never seen two people more in love and I was devastated when things didn't work out. Who knows, maybe there is still a future for the two of you after this case is over. I love you like a sister and I know that your lack of committing to anyone was due to the hurt you experienced with the end of your relationship with him, but I want to see you happy and Thomas or not, it's time you found that happiness."

Karen remained silent not wanting to admit that years didn't diminish her feelings for Thomas, but she needed to get them in check in order for her to do her job and do it well.

"This is probably my toughest case yet," she said instead of sharing about her feelings.

"You'll do fine. You were trained for this and if they didn't think you could do it, they wouldn't have you on it."

"Thanks for the vote of confidence. I can always count on you for support. I'm going to get back to this file. I still have a lot more to go over and I only have the weekend to get it done. Kiss the boys for me, tell Kevin I said hey and I'll talk to you Monday night."

"Okay. I love you girl," Lacey said.

"Love you back."

Karen felt better about the situation after talking to her best friend. Lacey knew the right things to say to help her relax and feel at ease. She took a bite of her sandwich and began reading through the many documents in the file once again.

She scanned a document she hadn't read before and discovered that Thomas had done extremely well for himself financially and that he was pretty well off. She remembered seeing pictures of the home he lived in right outside of Raleigh, which actually seemed more like an estate built for a king.

She scanned through other photos in the folder of properties he owned in Miami as well as in the Bahamas, where he was from. The house on that island was on the beach and it was magnificent in her eyes. They often talked during their many nights of lovemaking about spending lots of time on the beach because they shared a loved for the water and wanted their kids to learn to swim like fish.

Karen read further and found that though he wasn't married, he was never short on company when it came to beautiful women. She frowned then smiled seeing pictures of him with an actress or two on his arm, first feeling jealous and then remembering she could only be happy for him and his success even when it came to the company he kept. From his bright smile and demeanor, she knew he had to be living a happy life. It didn't appear that the falling out with her years ago, made him miss a beat when it came to finding happiness again and success appeared to be second nature to him. He had set out to be successful and made it his number one priority and it appeared he had done so.

Looking at even more information on Thomas, she noted that his mother was still alive and living in splendor in the Bahamas in a beautiful home he'd purchased for her. He never did know his father and Karen didn't see any mentioning of him in any of the information on Thomas' background, so she assumed he never did find him. There was a time when one priority for him was in locating his father. He had a name and no other information and she was able to see that the FBI couldn't find a record of him either. The only thing his mother could tell him was that she and his father had a week-long fling when he visited the island and it wasn't until after he had left and gone back to his life did she discover she was pregnant. His father never came back to the island as far as his mother knew and she never heard from him again.

Most of what she read in the file about his childhood she already knew. He was sent to live with relatives at a young age in Florida because his mother had a problem with drinking and couldn't take care of a growing young boy who was beginning to get in all kinds of trouble. Once he moved to Florida, he spent a few years living a good life with an aunt and uncle. Eventually, they moved to Raleigh because of his uncle's work. Thomas would spend the summers on the island with his mother and other family members, but would always return to his aunt and uncle when it was time for school.

When he graduated high school and his mother was free from alcohol abuse, he decided to stay with his aunt and uncle, who had no children and who had agreed to make sure he went to college and worked towards making a good life for himself.

Karen had met him during his sophomore year in high school when she was a cheerleader for the team and he was a member of the football team. She was surprised to see a few pictures of the two of them in the file as well. She shouldn't have been since she knew the FBI could find whatever information they needed and there was nothing private about her life and relationship with Thomas back then.

The photos they had of her were easy to acquire since they were all taken from the high school year book. Those were great times, she thought to herself. She and Thomas had done so many things together and her parents loved him and had hoped that one day they would marry and produce grandkids that she had no doubt her parents would have spoiled if they could, but that wasn't to be. Before she started feeling somber again, she continued her review of the information.

Moving ahead to more recent information on him, she found the background story for the cover for the undercover operation.

It was the current bookkeeper, who was pregnant, that came upon a ledger that she had never seen before. She had noticed that some of the figures weren't adding up. Though the company had a full financial staff which included three full time accountants, the bookkeeper was the eyes and ears for the top leadership of the company and was the direct line between the accounting office and leadership.

The accounting office focused on the company's records while she focused on more of the personal finances of the top leaders. It was a stressful job, but she knew that Thomas didn't want a whole lot of people with their eyes on his personal business. She knew he would always have someone much closer to him involved in that, which was why he always employed a personal bookkeeper and not just a financial team. Someone amongst the additional photos of employees she now perused had been stealing money and her gut told her that it wasn't Thomas, but she would find out who.

She had to figure out who it was that was stealing the money and whoever it was, was doing it without the accounting staff knowing about it, unless someone in that office was responsible or at least in on it.

After reading over everything the first time, she realized most of the focus was placed on Thomas as chief executive officer and chief financial officer. One of the first things she would do was have her assistant back at the office dig a little bit deeper into the backgrounds of the other leaders in the company, especially those on the board. She wanted to turn over every rock and find everyone's secrets and not just concentrate on Thomas. She knew beyond any doubt that he was innocent and so she needed to turn her attention to who else could be guilty. She knew Thomas had made many sacrifices over the years to build up his company and she knew he wouldn't risk it all by taking from his own employees. Someone he trusted was stabbing him in the back and she would do everything within her power to figure it out. She had a few days to get her act together because on Monday, she would once again come face to face with the man who still held her heart after all these years. After ten years, she was about to encounter Thomas Atwater again, the only man she'd ever loved.

4

Thomas Atwater wasn't sure how he was going to replace his bookkeeper with someone he trusted on such short notice. His current one, Anita, who had been with him since he'd opened his Raleigh office, was six months pregnant and according to her, she was pregnant with twins. She was having major complications and the doctor was putting her on bed rest until the babies were born. He thought he would have a few more months before he'd have to worry about her replacement while she was out.

She was planning to be out for three months, but now with the twins, she would first be out until they were born and then she wanted to take an additional six months off, something he hadn't planned for. He figured he could get by for a few months without a replacement, but now he was looking at possibly an entire year. It was time he looked for some help now and he would start by checking with a few of his friends for any recommendations for temporary help. His personal assistant was also his personal record keeper, so he knew the hire would have to be done by him and not by his human resources department. There weren't just office books that needed to be kept, but he liked having someone close enough to him to help look after his own financial records. Before he thought too long and hard about it, he shook it off to deal with it later.

It was Monday and after his morning five-mile run, he needed to stop in the office briefly before having lunch with a local organization that was looking to partner with his company to provide free after school tutoring for inner city youth. Whenever he was contacted by local organizations looking for assistance, especially groups that helped inner city children, he always dealt with them directly. It was important to him to give back and he did so as often as he could, to the right organizations.

While he spent the morning getting dressed for his run, he thought about how much he admired his bookkeeper. She and her husband had been trying for a few years to have children and he was just as excited as she was the day she came running into his office to say that she was finally pregnant. There were times when he saw co-workers and friends with their wives and kids and that made him remember how he didn't have either. He sacrificed all of that to have the kind of business he wanted and the life he was now living and it didn't escape him that he often wondered if the sacrifice was worth it. He thought back to his discussion with Sarah from the night before and realized he'd made a promise to her that he would not continue to dwell on it and already he'd broken that promise.

He had dated over the years, but nothing serious since his relationship from many years ago, ended badly. Now, years later, he wished he could have gone back and changed the decision he'd made. He hated remembering those days because thoughts of them reminded him of how long it took for him to get over Karen and the love they shared. He'd been so driven with dreams of success that he let that get in the way of happiness with the woman he loved. He would much rather forget the time in his life when he'd made the biggest mistake and it had cost him. Though his life was full and he was happy, he knew that he could have been happier with all that he has if it also included Karen.

His friends often joked that his business was his wife and all of his employees were his kids. It wasn't quite the same, but for now, it was all he had and he made the best of it. He did have his best friend, Preston's kids that he loved as if they were his own, but it still wasn't the same as having his own. At this stage, it's what he had to settle for.

He'd been so focused on business over the years that his personal life slipped by without him realizing he still had personal goals he never achieved and those personal goals like a wife and kids now crept into his thoughts often. Now was not the time as he turned his attention back to his morning routine and getting ready to head into the office.

**

Karen woke early Monday morning a little nervous, but very much ready for her chance meeting with Thomas. She fought with being happy or sad over not experiencing anymore spicy dreams starring him. Reviewing his file brought back memories that her traitorous body wouldn't allow her to put on the back burner anymore. The mere thought of him and her body was like a moth to a flame, longing for him even though he wasn't there.

She'd spent the better part of the weekend at home preparing herself psychologically for the assignment. She was glad she'd gotten up early so that she could spend some time taking one last look at the file on Thomas, knowing that lunch time would arrive soon enough and she'd have to make her way to the restaurant which was a part of the plan put in place to get the undercover operation going.

Timing was everything today and the local FBI office had made sure the person Thomas was to meet for lunch would not be showing up. They would have him call Thomas to cancel just as he was arriving at the restaurant. He had always been a creature of habit and she knew from her notes exactly where she would be sitting, which would be right in his line of sight. He had a habit of checking out everything around him, seeing who was sitting or walking nearby. When they were together, she often joked that he had a phobia about strangers being close to him. There would be no way he'd be able to miss seeing her based on where she was instructed to sit. The restaurant server, who was actually a plant, had already been told to sit her at a specific table and in the seat that would be facing Thomas' table. She was as ready as she would ever be, she thought, putting the file away and planning the encounter out in her head.

Nervous was an understatement for how she was feeling. She wasn't sure what her immediate reaction would be to seeing him in person after so many years. Time had been wonderful to Thomas and he was as handsome as ever.

From the pictures, she could see that he was still an avid fan of the gym due to the exquisite physique he still sported. She could see his muscles in one of the photos of him in a t-shirt while working out at a gym. It was clear, the FBI had him under surveillance because there were several shots of him unaware that he was being photographed.

Karen couldn't help letting her eyes scan down the picture of Thomas working out at the gym until her eyes landed on his powerful legs. She remembered the force behind those legs as he moved around her, inside her and under her and her sex jumped at the remembrance. She literally shook her head to try and remove all thoughts of their intimate time together so that she could focus on the task at hand. It was hard to do when she recalled how masterfully he took care of her needs, always putting her pleasure ahead of his own and making sure the experience was explosive every single time and explosive it was. Though she'd dated and had been intimate with men since him, none had ever taken her to the point of ecstasy that Thomas had. He was in a class all by himself when it came to pleasing women.

If she could get her mind off of him in that way, she may be able to get the job done that her director was expecting of her. It was time to get her body in check with her mind. She didn't have time to continue focusing on how good and delicious his kisses were or how he knew the right places on her body to touch or even the way he moved his hips when they made love, hitting the right spots that drove her mad with passion.

"Ugh," Karen said out loud. She was doing it again. In need of a cold shower to get her mind and body back on track, she headed for the shower.

**

Thomas arrived at the restaurant a little early for his lunch meeting. He was given his favorite table to await the arrival of the head of one of the local branches of the Boys & Girls Club of Raleigh. He had been waiting about fifteen minutes when his cell phone rang. He recognized the number as belonging to Phil, the man he was supposed to have the lunch meeting with.

"Phil, I'm here at the restaurant waiting on you," he said as soon as he answered.

"I have to apologize for the late notice, but I won't be able to make it. We have a crisis at the office and I need to take care of this which will most likely take the rest of the day to clear up. I'll have to reschedule if that's okay with you."

"No problem. Just reschedule whenever your time permits."

"Thanks, and go ahead and have lunch on me. I called the restaurant and asked them to put your lunch on my account. It's the least I can do for cancelling at the last minute," Phil said.

"No Phil, there's no need for that. I'm probably going to head out to get some work done and skip lunch, but I appreciate the offer. I'll wait to hear from you on a rescheduled date."

"Okay and thanks again and just in case you change your mind, don't forget, lunch is still on me today."

"I'll talk to you soon Phil."

Thomas hung up the phone at the exact moment that his stomach growled, reminding him that he hadn't eaten yet, so since he was already at his favorite restaurant, he decided to stay and have a quick lunch.

He was about to signal the waiter to bring him a menu when he looked up and saw a beautiful woman being seated at the table right across from him. He watched the confidence in her walk and of course the sway of her hips and any man would be blind to not see she was beautiful. He couldn't get a good look at her because the waiter was blocking most of his view, but he was happy when he was able to catch a quick glimpse as she sat down.

As the waiter walked away, he got an even better look at her and couldn't believe his eyes. He knew her and there was no way he would ever forget her. The beautiful woman was Karen Jacobs, the one and only woman he'd ever been deeply in love with, the woman he had just been thinking about the night before and even earlier that morning and she was sitting a few feet away from him. He couldn't help, but stare at her since the years had been extremely good to her. She was stunningly beautiful and he had a quick flash of them together.

He was not only shocked to see her sitting at the table right across from him, but he was captivated by the magnitude of her sheer beauty which had multiplied in the years since he'd last seen her.

Karen's dark brown, with streaks of light colors was swooped up with a few tendrils hanging down around her face. She no longer wore glasses as she had years ago, and even at a distance, her light brown eyes were shining like a light beacon. He couldn't see much of what she was wearing, but from the waste up, he could see that she'd stayed in great shape.

As he was checking her out and trying to get over

the fact that she was sitting right in front of him, she looked up and caught him staring at her. His heart stopped beating the moment their eyes met and he wondered if familiarity would set in for her; would she remember and recognize him. From the start, it appeared she hadn't recognized him as she smiled and looked away, only to turn her attention back to him when it registered who he was. Thomas saw copious amounts of emotions pass across her face as the dots connected and she too looked as surprised to see him as he was to see her.

Memories of their past continued to flood his mind and he cautiously waited to see if her reaction would turn to anger as she remembered that they did not end their relationship on the best of terms and he didn't want this to be an uncomfortable moment. He felt better when recognition set in and she smiled lightly. He hoped it was a sign that she didn't harbor any bad feelings about him and the choice he made to choose business over love. His last thought before deciding to get up and go over to speak was that he hoped she didn't smile and when he reached her table, decide to throw a glass of water in his face. That wouldn't be a good look for him at all.

Surprise and recognition were powerful, Karen thought the instant Thomas had seen her. She could feel his eyes piercing right through her. She pretended for a few moments to not notice him since playing it cool was the name of the game if things were going to work out the way she hoped. After what she thought was a suitable amount of time, she looked up and around her before settling her eyes on him and sure enough he was still staring at her. She waited a few minutes before looking way and then back at him with a show of recognition on her face. She wanted to be sure to demonstrate a sudden look of shock and awareness at seeing him again. She stayed away from any look of anger at his presence because, of course, the plan was for him to say something to her to start a conversation. She needed to look at him with friendliness and an open invitation, but she had to be sure and not go overboard.

Getting herself under control, she smiled lightly while continuing to look relaxed, comfortable and approachable, letting him make the move without it seeming obvious that she was baiting him. So far things were working according to the plan because the look on Thomas' face said that any minute, he would be making a move in her direction. She nervously watched as he slid his chair back without breaking eye contact with her and headed in her direction. She relaxed knowing the game was on.

Approaching her table, Thomas felt a stir with every step. He saw her smile at him, but that could mean anything. He wouldn't dare continue to sit as if he hadn't seen her. She'd recognized him also, so there was no need to behave like they hadn't seen each other. He made his way over to her to say hello.

"Hello Karen," he said using a deep yet soft voice so that only she could hear him.

"Hello Thomas," was all she said since she wanted him to take the lead.

"You look beautiful and I must say I'm shocked to see you here. It's been a long time."

"Thank you and yes it has been a very long time. How have you been?"

"I've been great. Are you dining alone? I don't want to intrude or anything."

"Yes, I am actually. I was doing some window shopping in the area and heard this was a great place for lunch, so I decided to stop in and grab a bite to eat. What about you? Am I keeping you from a lunch guest?" she said making sure to add animation to the moment by look back at his table as if she was looking for someone else to appear.

Thomas didn't register what she was saying. He was more focused on the red of her lips and the fact that her lips were moving so perfectly, he forgot to pay attention to the words coming out of them.

"No, not at all. In fact, I was supposed to have a business meeting over lunch, but he called and cancelled."

"Oh, I hope your friend is okay."

"Yes, he's fine. It was something small."

Silence ensued as they stared at each other, forgetting everything else that was going on around them. It became awkward after a few moments of him standing beside her table without sitting or leaving.

"Since we're both dining alone, would you mind if I joined you or you could join me at my table? I'd love to sit and talk and do a little catching up, that is if you have the time."

"No, I don't mind at all. Why don't you join me," she said, glad he was making all of the moves.

Thomas took his seat and signaled his waiter to inform him he would be moving. Now that they were sitting right across from each other, he wasn't sure of what to say.

He wanted to know everything about her life since he'd last seen her, but he didn't want to seem too eager.

"So, tell me what brings you to Raleigh, Karen? Last I heard you had moved to the west coast quite a few years back?"

Karen relaxed and fell comfortably in the conversation.

"Yes, I did, but I recently moved back here. I'm living in my parents' old house."

Karen was now living back in the house where he's spent a lot of his time, he thought. She was no longer thousands of miles away.

"I didn't realize you still owned that house."

"The next-door neighbor has been taking care of it all of these years. It had been rented out a few times, but for the past two years, I've left it empty."

"What brought you back to the area?" he

inquired, still shocked that she was living back in the area.

"Well, I was tired of living in Seattle. It rains too much and at first I thought I wanted something new, a new area, a new environment and then I realized what I really needed was something old and sentimental. I decided until I really figured out what I wanted to do, I might as well come back home for a while. I invested the money well that was left to me by my parents and I saved quite a bit over the years, so I gave my notice at my company and moved back here to relax before diving back in to figure out what I really want to do with my life from this point on. I was thinking of starting my own accounting firm or something along that line, but I don't really know yet."

Karen wanted to get a few questions in also about his life over the years to see if it matched up with what she'd read in the files.

"So, what have you been up to these past few years Thomas?" she asked.

The waiter showed up to take their lunch orders and when he'd retreated once again, Thomas settled in to bring Karen up to date on his life.

"Well, after I left Raleigh, I lived in New York for a few years. I took that time to learn about the world of finance and when the opportunity arose, I was able to expand even more on the company I eventually started here in Raleigh after working all those years in New York under some of the biggest and most successful people in the world of finance. I had taken over the reins of a company in New York and when the chance for me to make that company all mine, I did and moved my operations back here to Raleigh, merging with a financial firm I took over here which led to where I am today."

"So, you chose to move back here to Raleigh to run your business and not stay in the very popular New York business district?"

"Yes, even though that wasn't my original plan. I thought about staying there, but I grew up in this area and if I could have a hand in building it up, I was going to do that. Some of the employees from New York who wanted to stay with the company came with me to Raleigh and I was able to keep everyone on board in the company I took over here in town. The majority of my staff are from right here in this area and I'm working with other companies to bring more businesses into the area. I've always had plans to return to Raleigh once I knew it was time to do so. My heart will always be right here in Raleigh. I have smaller branches of my company in several other states, but they are all connected to the main office right here."

Karen didn't know that. She remembered his wanting to leave to pursue opportunities, but she remembered in the heat of the argument the last time they had spoken that he wanted to move to New York and wanted her to go with him, but she declined. After that, there were no more discussion and he'd left after not choosing her and neither one of them looked back. Karen looked at Thomas and could see he must have been reliving the same last moments of the last conversation they'd had just as she was. The mentioning of New York took them both back to that night.

The moment with him was more intense than she thought it would be. Their eyes met and connected and they'd smile and look away, only to come back to gazing at each other again with no words being exchanged.

"Karen, I'm sorry for what happened in the past. I hope you believe that. We were young and I was hungry for fortune and the life I'd built up for myself in my mind. It wasn't that I didn't love you, but I was driven and like an idiot, it played a bigger role in the plan for my life than love."

Karen didn't want to have that conversation. She needed to get the conversation back to the present. Seeing him was having a bigger emotional impact on her than she thought and all of the old memories were making her feel melancholy and that had no place in the job she had to do. She also couldn't dismiss what he'd just revealed, so she responded in hopes of moving beyond the trip down this emotional lane.

"Thomas, it's okay, really it is. I know that it's old news and clearly, we both survived it and are doing great. There is nothing to apologize for since you had a right to live the life you wanted to live back then and now."

She hoped that would be the last of the good old days that they would be discussing today. She couldn't handle much more of it. Though her face and words were clear that she was okay, inside she wasn't. Sitting across from him brought back many memories, some good and bad. She didn't need to add to it by taking more trips down memory lane; she needed to focus on her task. She knew that any minute another part of the plan would unfold. It began just as Thomas was about to ask her another question. He was halted by the presence of a friend of his stopping by the table. This was not just any friend, but it was the husband of his bookkeeper. This, she knew, as also a part of the plan.

"Stan," Thomas greeted him as he stepped over to the table.

"Thomas, it's good to see you."

"How's Anita doing? What about the babies?" Thomas inquired.

"She's doing good, so far. Since Friday, she's been taking it easy and resting in bed and the babies are good. The doctor wants her off of her feet as much as possible so that she can carry them as close to her due date as possible. Sorry she had to leave you in a lurch with the job."

"It's no problem. I know how long you've been wanting to have children."

Stan looked over at Karen.

"Oh, Stanley Harlen, this is Karen..." he looked

at her to confirm her last name, "Is it still Jacobs?"

She nodded.

"Yes, it is," she said. The little response held a lot of weight. For the first time, she thought about the fact that she hadn't lived much of the life they would talk about back when they were together. A big part of that was getting married and having children. They both wanted a big family, yet neither of them were married with children.

"This is Karen Jacobs. She grew up here in Raleigh and recently moved back to the area," Thomas said.

"Nice to meet you Karen."

"Likewise," she replied.

"Well, I won't keep you from your lunch. I saw you when I came in to grab some takeout for Anita. You know you turned her on to the shrimp and chicken salad at this place."

"Well make sure you tell her I was thinking about her and if I can do anything for you guys, just let me know."

"We appreciate that Thomas. I'll be sure to keep you posted on how things progress with her. In the meantime, I hope you won't have a hard time finding a replacement for her at least until she returns to work."

"I'll be working on that this week actually. Anita will be a hard act to follow, but thankfully it's only temporary. Her job will be waiting for her when she's ready to come back."

"I'll be seeing you," Stan said as he walked away.

Perfect, Karen thought to herself. Things played out just as she was told they would. Now, she needed to turn the conversation to the job that Stanley Harland had brought up. They played that very well, she thought of her FBI team.

"So, what's this I hear about you being in a lurch about something? Am I prying if I ask about that?" she asked as if she didn't already know.

"No, not at all. My bookkeeper has been trying to get pregnant for a few years now. A few months ago, she found out she was pregnant and more recently discovered it was twins. She started having some problems and her doctor told her if she wanted to carry the babies to term, she needed to be off of her feet, taking it easy until they're born. That left me without a bookkeeper and she's been with me since I came back to this area. I'm going to begin my search this week for a temporary replacement until she returns from maternity leave in about a year."

"You don't have a full accounting staff on board for a company your size?" she inquired. Karen knew she needed him to tell her everything.

"Yes, I do. I like for them to focus their interest on the company while the bookkeeper focuses most of her attention on my personal records and accounts and some business aspects as well. I like to have as few people as possible with their eyes on my finances."

Karen understood that. She remembered a lot of things about Thomas and that was one she was sure of. He liked to keep as much of his life as private as he possibly could.

"So, Karen, tell me what have you been doing with yourself besides working? Did you ever get married or have any children?"

Thomas waited on pins, nervous about whether she had found her prince charming after they parted or if she'd had any children. He knew how much she wanted both. He'd lost touch of her and though she hadn't already mentioned any children, that didn't mean she didn't have any.

"No, I never married, nor do I have any children. What about you?"

"No wife or children for me either. I've been pretty much married to my business all of these years."

"Well besides not finding a husband or having any children, I have been busy at work over the years. I was most recently employed as a senior accountant. You know how much I love numbers."

Thomas did remember that about her.

"Yes, I do remember that," he chuckled.

"What I plan to do now is spend some time getting comfortable back in the area. I don't plan to engross myself into another full-time job any time soon. I'll probably take on some freelance type accounting work for a while just to keep my skills sharp. My investments have really paid off and I'm thankful I don't have to run out and find a job right away."

Lunch arrived and they started eating and uncomfortable silence invaded their space once again. Karen was hoping Thomas would take the bait about her only wanting to do some work occasionally and that he would consider asking her if she was interested in a little part time work for his company. They still had to get through lunch and she hoped by the time it ended, that the thought would at least have entered his mind, even if he didn't ask her about it today.

"So, Karen, would I be insulting you in any way if I said if you're looking for something to do to keep your skills on point, that you could do some part time work at Atwater Industries? You could work as few or as many hours as you'd like and at the same time, I wouldn't have to try so hard to find a replacement for my bookkeeper."

Jackpot, Karen thought. He walked right into it.

She thought for a few minutes before she spoke, tampering down her desire to immediately say yes, by pretending to chop her salad and sported a serious look on her face as if she were seriously considering what he was saying.

"You mean come to work for you? No, Thomas, that wouldn't be insulting at all. Are you sure you really want to do that?"

She looked up at him hoping that last line didn't make him doubt asking her.

"I've never been more sure. Again, you can plan out our own work schedule and you can also do some work from home. With your know-how with money and numbers, my need for help right now and your desire to find something occasional to keep your accounting mind fresh, I think it would be great," Thomas admitted.

Karen ate a little of her salad and acted as if she were really thinking it over before answering.

"I think it sounds pretty good to me too, but can I get back to you by the end of the day tomorrow?"

"Absolutely. I'll give you my card and after you think about it, give me a call and let me know your decision."

They continued eating and catching up and she even gave him the rundown on Lacey and her family. Back in the day, they had all been friends. When lunch was finally over and Karen had achieved what she set out to, she prepared to leave.

"Well Thomas it was great seeing you again."

She reached for her wallet to cover her portion of the meal.

Thomas stopped her.

"This lunch is on me. It's been so good seeing you again and I'm glad we were able to put the past behind us and are able to sit across the table from each other and talk."

"So am I. That was a long time ago and there is no need to harbor any resentment after all of these years," she said.

The truth was, putting aside the work reason, she really was glad to see him again and to know that he was doing okay.

"Thank you for sharing lunch with me," Thomas said. He hated that their lunch had to end, but he had a few things to do himself.

"Thank you for lunch. I have quite a few more things to do today and I'm still getting settled in at the house, but I promise I'll get right back to you on the job offer."

Thomas stood as soon as she did.

"I'll walk you out," he said after leaving the money for their meal along with a very generous tip.

Thomas came around as she stood and helped her with her jacket. The light touch of his hand on her shoulder made her shiver slightly. Job or no job, she recognized signs of trouble and I had nothing to do with her assignment. She knew the meaning of that shiver and it told her that she wanted him and with that thought, she knew she was in trouble.

5

Driving was more difficult than Karen had anticipated especially when she was trying to hold her composure until she had driven far enough away that no one would be able to see her come apart. Her hands were shaking, she broke out in a sweat and her legs were experiencing a nervous twitch and if she didn't pull over soon, she would have an accident. She remembered a little turn-off that led to a private road coming up and she took that path because getting out of the car to exhale was a priority.

As her car came to a stop, Karen looked around and seeing no one, she stepped out and tried to take in as much air as she could. She paced back and forth beside the car until her heart slowed down and she could breathe comfortably again. This job was going to be harder than she thought.

She had been fine sitting across from Thomas throughout lunch, but as soon as she got in the car, the weight of seeing him again and the memories of their past hit her hard and she felt like she couldn't breathe.

She didn't realize the impact of seeing Thomas in person again would have on her. A startling wave of remembrance overwhelmed her when he first approached the table. She tried her best to shield her reaction to him and prayed that she was successful. Her thoughts were all over the place as soon as she saw him stand and recognized the physique that she once loved being up against. He looked good, as he always had, but even more so as he'd gotten older. He had the kind of body that was meant to be worshipped and she remembered many nights of doing just that. Even now her body began to shudder and throb at the thought of the many nights she'd spent pleasing that body.

Thomas had been her first, teaching her how he liked to be pleased and she was more than ready to oblige him every chance she got. Those thoughts flooded her mind every time he opened his mouth to utter a word. She remembered what it felt like to have that mouth on her body and how he never missed an opportunity to cover every single inch, not just with his lips, but with his tongue, all the while driving her to the brink of insanity with anticipation of the orgasm she knew was on its way, providing her with pleasure she wanted to prolong while at the same time, looking forward to the exhilarating feeling of the powerful release.

Karen leaned back against the car as her mind played like a movie showing her full color images of her time with him. One time in particular she remembered they couldn't wait to get back to his apartment. Halfway through a movie that had turned them both on, they got up and left without saying a word knowing what was next. Thomas had driven them to his place with lightning speed and once there, before she had a chance to lock the door behind them, he'd pressed her up against the nearest wall.

Karen snapped out of her thoughts and got back in her car. She wasn't helping her body calm down by remembering that steamy night. She turned the car on and started the air to quickly cool off her heated skin. As she leaned back while the cool air soothed her, she couldn't stop thinking about that night once again.

After Thomas leaned her against the wall, he'd slowly slid her arms above her head and told her to keep them there as he slid down her body stopping long enough to unbutton her top and without taking her bra off, he slid her mounds out from under the cups and sucked first one and then the other nipple gently into his mouth soothing the hard tips with his tongue. With that same tongue, he made a path down her stomach until he encountered the top of her pants. She waited with anticipation knowing that his next move would be to remove them so that he could quickly sheath himself and give them both the relief they sought. Thomas surprised her when all he did was unsnap and then unzip her pants. He stood to his full length and whispered naughty things in her ear as he slid his hand past the barrier of her panties right to that part of her that longed for his touch the most. When he encountered her essence and the wetness that flowed down his fingers, his excitement heightened enjoying how turned on she was for him.

Karen had been on the brink of losing her mind when he used a single finger to spread her essence all around before using that same finger to enter her where he found it easy to do because of how slippery her passage way had been. As he continued to whisper and tell her all of the things he wanted to do to her and what he wanted her to do to him, her hips developed a mind of their own as she ground them in short circles to get more out of his strokes. When Thomas then used his thumb to stroke her hard nub, he added two more fingers and the feeling was more than she could take. He nibbled on her earlobe, an act he knew would be her undoing and when she soared over the edge, his strokes became fierce in their attempt to prolong her orgasm, which to her, went on and on as if there would be no end to it. She screamed out her pleasure not caring if she'd wake his neighbors or not. She was so hot for him and didn't care who knew.

Just as her body began calming down, Thomas didn't give her long to catch her breath as she leaned against him exhausted from wave after wave of pleasure that she'd encountered. Before she knew what was happening, he lifted her up off of her feet and slid down to the carpeted floor. When he knew that she was in a comfortable position, he removed her clothing and did the same with his own. He quickly sheathed himself with protection they always made sure they had with them and before her next breath, he had opened her legs, planted himself at her center and in one slow surge forward, he entered her body ever so sweetly, taking her next breath away.

Thomas was a thorough lover and that night was no exception. He drove into her slowly at first while planting kisses across her face and neck, telling her how good she felt encasing him with her softness. His slow rocks into her quickly turned into deep thrusts as she held on for the ride of her life. He whispered his love for her over and over again while calling her name and when her hips began matching his thrusts, he increased the pace. The feel of him sliding in and out of her pliant body with his hardened flesh was just enough to send her once again over the edge and this time he followed her, shouting out his own release as he steamrolled like a piston into her. Where she thought she was coming down from her explosion, once again she was thrown into another orgasm. She held on to Thomas, never wanting him to stop giving her all of him. Their lovemaking was magical like that each and every time and she never thought she'd get enough of him.

Still sitting in her car, Karen looked down when realized she had reached up and began caressing her breasts through the opening of her blouse and stopped herself. She sat straight up in her car and looked around to be sure no one had come up to her car while she'd been thinking about them in the throes of passion. She removed her hands from her breasts and shook her head to gather her thoughts. She couldn't do this to herself. She had to forget about their past, especially those times when they were intimate. This was going to end up being the roadblock to her finding the truth about what was going on at Atwater Industries and though she and Thomas had a past, she had a job to do.

It was obvious to her that the intense connection they once shared was still there. She felt it and she had a feeling Thomas had felt it as well, even though they both did a great job of keeping their cool. There was a look he would often get in his eyes that told her he wanted her and she saw that look staring back at her even though she tried to pretend as if it didn't have an impact on her. Obviously, it did because she was sitting in her car about to have an orgasm from a memory. Now was not the time to allow her body to control her every time she encountered Thomas Atwater. Her job and his livelihood depended on it.

Karen took several breaths, started the car and

headed home. She had a report to file about how well things went at the restaurant. Her boss would be eager to get her feedback and she needed to get into another cold shower. She had a feeling she would be taking lots of those. To get her mind off of Thomas, she called Lacey to tell her about her encounter with him knowing that her friend was anxiously waiting by the phone for her call. It was no surprise to her when Lacey answered on the first ring.

"Karen, I was hoping you would call. So, how was it? Did you want to rip his clothes off right there at the table? Was it love at first sight again? Did you wear something sexy that left his mouth watering? I need details!"

Karen shook her head. Leave it to her to turn something business into a prelude for sex.

"Well, hello to you too, Lace."

She heard Lacey laugh out loud on the other end.

"Oh right, I forgot that part. Okay, let me start over. Hey, Karen, how are you? How was lunch? Did you want to rip his clothes off right at the table? Was it love at first sight again? Did you dress sexy? Come on girl, I need the details!" she exclaimed loudly enough that Karen had to turn the volume down on her Bluetooth.

"Real funny Lace and calm down because you know that the lunch was all about business. No sexual innuendos please and things were quite civil. I did, however, want to tell you how it went if you'd like to hear that part of it."

Karen could hear her friend sigh on the other end of the phone.

"Okay, if you must share about business. As your friend, I'm required to listen, so shoot," she quipped.

"Well for starters, everything worked out according to the plan. He did end up talking to me about the bookkeeper position. I told him I would get back to him sometime tomorrow after I've had time to think about it. Of course, I'm going to take it since that was the purpose for the whole scenario. Taking the job will give me a chance to actually talk to the key people at the company to try and get a feel for who may have something to hide."

Karen continued telling Lacey about the meeting and tried as much as she could to stay away from telling her how good he looked and how much she did want to rip his clothes off and jump him right there on the spot. She could tell Lacey was trying to be supportive as she had always been, but she also knew that it was the good, juicy stuff that she really wanted to hear about.

"Now to satisfy your inquiring mind, he is still as delectable in person as he ever was and all I could think about was ripping every stitch of clothing off of his gorgeous body and giving those people at the restaurant a front row view of what it's like to be a woman who hasn't had any in a long time, but I digressed and kept it all about business," she said laughing when she heard Lacey curse.

"Kay, I know you're keeping this light and I like that you can find the fun in this, but be careful. Not just with the job you have to do, but with your heart. I know you said that to wet my whistle, but make sure you don't let your old feelings get in the way of who the new Thomas may be. I know he's scrumptious and all and we both know he had a way of playing you like a well-tuned piano, but remember to keep those feelings separate. I'm glad you got that first interaction out of the way and you know I'm hoping that after all of this is over, you and Thomas can find your way back to each other. I know the FBI picked you for this case because of your past with him and their reasons suck in my book, but watch your back because we both know Thomas isn't doing this, but whoever is doing it, is setting Thomas up for this fall and it could be dangerous."

"I know Lace and I will. I'm heading back to the house now to send my report through to the office and check in and do some thinking about my game plan. I'll be fine and I know what you're saying. I don't think there is anything in the cards for Thomas and I on a personal level anymore because I think too much time has passed. I still find him attractive and as debonair as ever, but that isn't enough for me anymore. He's still just as driven as he ever was and I remember what that did to me years ago and the one thing I won't do is allow him to do it to me again. When this case is over, I'm going home and he'll be able to get back to the life he lives this time without the FBI watching him day and night. Thanks for always being an ear and I admit, once I left the restaurant, I got swept up in my feelings from long ago, but I won't let those thoughts cloud my judgement. Kiss the boys for me and I'll give you a call later this week."

After the call ended, she thought about Lacey's concern and she was right. She needed to be careful and telling that to herself, she wasn't just talking about the job, but she was also talking about her heart. The way her heart raced after seeing him again was not a good sign for her trying to keep things about business. Thinking hard about her plan to keep things strictly business had to be her only focus.

6

Concentration didn't come easy for Thomas after seeing Karen. He entered his home and headed straight to his bar to get a drink. He never drank in the middle of the day, but today was not like any other day. Today, he had come face to face with the one woman he had never been able to forget about and it didn't matter how many women he'd been with over the years and there had been plenty.

His mind had been troubled with thoughts of her ever since he left her in the parking lot of the restaurant. It had been a total shock seeing her again though he'd thought about her a lot over the years. Never in his wildest dreams would he have thought that she would be back in Raleigh and sitting at the table across from him looking like a vision of beauty out of one of his dreams.

For years, when he dreamt of her, he would see her as he'd last seen her, young, beautiful and sexy. Now his thoughts were filled with her being older, more beautiful and even more sexier. He could remember a time when they were wild for each other. Whenever they got together, they couldn't keep their hands off of each other. Clothes, hands and kisses would fly in all directions as they raced toward the ultimate mental, emotional and physical connection.

Karen was the first and only woman he'd ever been in love with and seeing her today confirmed that was still the case. Seeing her again gave him vivid memories of many days and nights they had spent caressing, kissing and loving each other to fulfillment. She was not only still as sexy as ever, but he never thought that she could be any more beautiful than he remembered, but she proved him wrong because today she was stunning.

Thomas drank his drink like a starving man as he realized he'd made the craziest move without thinking by offering her a job. Of all people, he offered Karen Jacobs, the woman he'd devastated in the past by not choosing her, a job. At the time, all he could think about was seeing her again and that was the only way he could think of to make that happen without actually asking her out on a date, something he knew she would probably decline. He hoped she would take the job because even though they had a bad breakup, there was no one he would trust more with his finances than her.

Thomas thought back to a time when he'd first laid eyes on her as a young boy and even then, he knew she'd be his. He still chastised himself for making the mistake of not choosing her.

As the years went by and they grew closer and gave their virginity to each other, he knew she was made for him. Today, he realized he still loved her and that love helped him realize what was missing from his life and it wasn't just having a family, a wife and kids, but it was Karen. If he knew of a way to fix what he destroyed in the past and prove to her that she was worthy of being first in his life, he would do it and not think twice. Right after they'd said hello again, he was a goner. Knowing that she wasn't and had not married nor had any children was a sign that they were made for each other. At least that was what he told himself.

Neither of them had found that person to replace the love they had for each other. Now he needed to find a way to make that happen again. The best part of all of this was he was going to get the chance to do so because fate had landed at his doorstep the moment she moved back into town. He wasn't going to mess up this time if given the opportunity.

Now that he was home for the rest of the day, he had nothing but time on his hands. He checked his schedule and nothing had been added and though there were a few messages he needed to return, he wasn't planning to do that. He was going to do what he set out to do and that was to enjoy some time at home relaxing.

Thomas grabbed the rest of his drink and went into his media room, turned on the television that completely covered the wall and sat back in one of his theater style chairs. He flipped through the channels where nothing seemed to interest him and as hard as he tried, his thoughts still turned to Karen. He couldn't seem to shake the image of her sitting, smiling and laughing across from him. He missed the days of old when they would have dinner like that and then return to his place for a night of lovemaking. Images of one of the last nights they were together at his place came into focus and his attention turned away from the television.

They had spent the evening making love in front of the fireplace in his apartment. That evening's love fest began playing in his mind, vivid and clear like it had just happened.

"So, are we going to spend the entire night together tonight? Where is your mother?" Thomas said while seductively kissing Karen across the back of her neck. He had learned her body and its reaction and he knew that this one act would be the start of a night of uninhibited love.

"Mmm, yes we are going to be together all night long," Karen replied on a sigh, enjoying the feel of Thomas kissing and caressing her neck which she knew, as he did, it was all that was needed to get her in the mood.

"She went to visit her sister. She'll be back in a few days, so you have me all to yourself tonight and I'm wondering what will you do with me."

They were sitting on the floor in front of the

fireplace with the fire being the only light in the room. Thomas had purposely set the scene for a night of romance and when his mouth moved down the side of her neck, Karen didn't want to take things slow anymore. She needed him inside of her. She needed him to join their bodies and help her relieve the pressure that was building. She was sitting with her back to him in between his legs, feeling his strong, pulsating, hard and ever growing flesh increasing in size against her back as he continued his kisses and caresses. She could tell that he didn't want to rush things. Tonight, he wanted nice and slow and for him, she would do anything, even the nice and slow, so she closed her eyes and leaned into him enjoying his play of unhurried seduction.

Thomas could see there was no need for any more talking. All he wanted at this point was for her to feel. As he continued kissing around her neck and shoulder blades, he felt her squirming against him, a clear sign to him that that she was more than ready for more.

This is how he wanted things to always be between them. He looked forward to a lifetime of sharing exactly as they were now. He loved Karen with a deepness he never thought he'd experience and with the work schedule he maintained, times like this night were rare and he didn't want it to go by too fast.

When Karen leaned her head back on his

shoulder, he reached his hands down to draw her skirt further up her legs so that he could softly caress her thighs. His strong, brittle hands encountered goose bumps that had begun to form from his light touch. Thomas took his time pulling her legs further apart until each one crossed over the outside of his, leaving her center open for his touch.

As his hands traveled further into the apex of her thighs, he smiled when Karen presented him with a lust-filled moan that traveled through his body making him even harder, if that were even humanly possible because he was struggling with being painfully, but pleasantly harder than he'd ever been in his life. In his desire to torture her, he was torturing himself and hoped he could last through his plan of seduction like nothing Karen had ever experienced with him. There was no television playing, no music in the background and the only sound in the room were of their moans of pleasure which filled the air and added to the strength of the connection they shared.

As his hands finally reached her sweetest spot, he traced the band of lace around the outside of her panties driving her wild. Karen writhed under his ministrations even more trying to direct him where she needed him the most.

"I need you Thomas, so no more teasing, please. I need you right now. I can't take anymore," she whispered.

"Shhh, no more talking. The only thing I want you to do is feel and I know your body and believe me, you can take much more."

Thomas didn't prolong her pleasure as he moved his fingers beyond the only barrier between his fingers and what he knew was soaking wet and waiting for his touch. When his right hand cupped her mound, his marauding finger dipped inside of her while he used his left hand to caress her breast through her top. The dual assault turned Karen's moaning into screams of pleasure as he continued his caresses, watching her sizzle as hot as the flame coming from the fireplace.

As he suspected, he could feel Karen as she reached for her release. He had to hold her body in place with his legs or she would have leaped from his embrace when her orgasm slammed into her as if she had been zapped by lightening. She screamed and squirmed through her release and he refused to give up on his stroke. He wanted her to have this and he enjoyed having her come apart in his arms.

When her release began to subside, Thomas reluctantly pulled his hand from in between her legs and whispered his undying love to her as her body calmed from his touch.

Karen finally turned in his embraced and took his lips in a searing kiss that let him know she appreciated the level of attention he'd paid to her, making sure, as he always did, that she took her *pleasure first.*

As she turned in his arms, he felt her hands as they splayed across the hard ridge of his erection which appeared to be bursting at the seam behind his zipper. His breath quickened when she slowly unzipped him, taking great care not to hurt his bulging flesh. In an instant, he reached into his pocket for protection, barely able to hold on until he joined them together as one. They didn't worry about the fact that they were both still fully clothed. Instead, he covered his waiting flesh and when it was in place, he lifted Karen up, not breaking the kiss, slid her panties to the side and after lifting her high, he brought her down in one long plunge on his rock-hard member in an act that felt like home, a place where he would never tire of being.

Thomas broke the kiss to breathe through the sensual haze that was surrounding them as he plunged up into her over and over again while continuing to guide her up and down over him again and again. He lifted her up until only the tip of him remained inside and then bringing her back down until she was seated on him all the way to the base drove them both wild. He felt her rising again to where her release was once again within reach and he knew she was ready to explode. Thomas welcomed that because he was right there with her. They were making their own version of a blazing, hot, burning fire.

Thomas was breathing erratically, but kept up the pace.

"With me this time Karen," he shouted, about to lose control. Together they tumbled as he stroked in and out of her channel as her body tightened around him. They rode out the pleasure together as she contracted around him while he groaned through his own release which rocked his body to its core. They remained that way as their bodies calmed, neither wanting to move or break the intimate connection.

Thomas knew that a trip down memory lane is not what he needed right now as the ringing of his phone startled him back to the present. He looked at it to see that it was his assistant calling from the office. It must be important if she were calling his cell. He answered before it went to voice mail, not missing the fact that he was now somehow standing in the middle of the room with a hard-on, unmatched to any he'd had since Karen. She was still deeply rooted into his system and he wasn't sure that'd he made a good decision offering her a job, especially if she decided to accept it. He would have to be around her all the time. He was the CEO of his company and the last thing he needed to do was walk around all day with a stiffy every time he saw her. He would have to survive each encounter knowing what was underneath her clothes which was a sexy body that could bring him pleasure over and over again.

Thomas took the call from his assistant and refocused to calm his body. Perhaps Karen wouldn't accept the job offer and save him from the torture of seeing her each day while not being able to have her. After what he'd done to her, he knew she would never forgive him and he was sure she hadn't forgotten that last day together. There is nothing he could do about their past, but he wanted to do something about their present by showing her how sorry he was for the way things ended for them and maybe, just maybe, he could fight to get back what the biggest mistake he'd ever made had cost him; the love of his life. They had the kind of love that should have lasted a lifetime. If he could get any of that back, he was planning to do so. Fate had stepped in to give him a chance to make it right and he planned on doing that.

7

Agreeing to work in the office three days a week for eight hours a day turned out to be a great idea, Karen thought to herself. It was her first full day and it was going to be spent with Thomas, finding out exactly what he wanted her to do.

One day after Thomas made her the offer, she'd called him to accept the temporary position. Everything was falling into place and she only hoped she'd endure being in constant contact with him.

She had spent the night before unable to sleep as her mind and body stayed on Thomas. As much as she would like to hate him for how he'd left her years ago, she still loved him and there was no getting around that. The way Thomas had looked at her as they sat across from each other showed that there was no doubt that he still had feelings for her too. She won't say love, but she definitely saw lust. She was glad that she was able to keep the conversation short when she called to let him know she would be accepting the position. He sounded happy to hear from her and to know that she was big enough to take the job while leaving their history in the past.

Now up and at the office bright and early, she was ready to meet everyone on the staff that reported directly to him, including the entire accounting staff. With the amount of money that was alleged to have been stolen, someone in accounting had to be in on it. It had to be someone in accounting assisting someone on the executive level and no matter how many times her boss tried to convince her that Thomas was the likely choice, she wasn't buying it, though she wouldn't let him in on her suspicions of another person. She knew if she took Thomas' side, everyone at her office would assume it was because of their history together and she may get pulled from the case. Another agent wouldn't look in another direction and she'd lose her chance to prove that Thomas was not a thief.

The average employee wouldn't have access to steal a large amount of money and keep it hidden from everyone at the top. The person or persons responsible had to be close to Thomas to be able to pin the trail of the stolen money on him and get away with it. She would find out who it was and clear Thomas' name before the FBI swooped in and arrested him.

She entered the office that had been assigned to her and had just sat down when she looked up to see Thomas standing in the doorway looking as sexy as ever, even at an early hour of the morning.

"Good morning, Karen."

"Hi, Thomas."

Karen noted the soft and sexy tone of her response and vowed to fix that to keep everything about business.

"I hope you're settling in okay. I understand from human resources that you've done all of your paperwork and everything is all good."

"Yes, I received most of the documents by email yesterday and I completed everything and dropped them off with them when I got here this morning. This is a very nice office building you have. It doesn't look this massive from the outside. You've done well for yourself and I'm sure you're proud of the sacrifices you've made over the years to get here."

Thomas thought about that before replying, never taking his eyes off of hers even for a second. He wanted her to read between the lines of his response.

"Not all of the sacrifices were worth it, but that was then and this is now and yes, I'm happy in my life, but I still wonder if I could have been happier with a few different choices."

Karen knew what Thomas was trying to say without actually saying it and she let his words hang in the air. Now wasn't the time to go down that rabbit's hole. She refocused the conversation back to business.

"This building and the business are a great testament to your dedication to getting what you desire."

Not all of it, he thought to himself. He was looking at his greatest desire and yet it wasn't his.

"Thank you. It took a lot of hard work and dedication and I'm proud of it. Listen, there is a meeting this morning I want you to come to. It will give you a chance to meet everyone, especially the accounting staff that you'll work closely with. I also want you to meet the other officers in the company. It just so happens that they are all here this week though most travel often. I've briefed everyone about you starting here today and about your background in accounting. To say they were impressed would be an understatement and they were happy to hear I was able to get you to start so quickly."

Karen listened as he came further into her office and closed the door.

Thomas sauntered up to her desk so that if anyone walking by her office knew that they were talking, they couldn't hear what he was saying.

"What I didn't do was tell them anything about our past other than we grew up together. I didn't want things to be awkward for you or for them. I didn't want you to think that I didn't share that because I didn't want to remember that time in my life, but I want to be sure you are comfortable being here without people getting too personal too fast about something that really is none of their business."

Karen respected that. Though the job was a front for the main reason she was there, she wanted to avoid any real awkward moments because of her connection to him.

"Thanks Thomas and I do appreciate that. It will help me a great deal in getting my job done if anything personal about our history stayed between you and I."

He smiled and her heart melted a little more.

"That's great to hear. The meeting starts in thirty minutes and I'll send my assistant in to get you before the meeting starts to be sure you can find your way to the conference room."

"Sounds like a plan and I am looking forward to meeting everyone," she said.

"Well, I'll let you get settled in since I see you've been given the company manual to read through on your first day. It's a lot of material about the history of the company and my vision for it, but don't feel obligated to read it all today. I better head out to prepare for the meeting and I guess I'll see you there."

Karen nodded and reached for the book as he turned to leave. She needed to look anywhere, but at Thomas. Her heart was already racing not knowing what he was going to say when he'd entered and shut the door. She didn't know what to accept, but to herself, she had hoped for something more personal. She was glad when that didn't occur. At least one of them was keeping things on a business level. She was failing miserably.

"Oh, and Karen?"

She looked at him questionably.

"Yes?"

He hesitated before continuing, not wanting to make her feel uncomfortable, but not being able to resist.

"You look beautiful this morning."

She blushed when his compliment caught her off guard. She stuttered through her response as her two-timing body trembled at the deep tone of his voice and the piercing stare of eyes she remembered looking into many times as they made love. Why couldn't her body play fair and not react this way to him? She thought.

"Thank you very much."

Thomas didn't say anything else as he nodded and exited her office.

After he was gone, she fell back against the soft back of the leather chair and exhaled. This was going to be harder than she thought.

**

"Good morning everyone."

Karen looked up at the sound of Thomas' voice as he addressed the staff that were gathered around the conference table for the early morning meeting. Her heart rate increased seeing him in a charcoal gray suit that had been tailor made just for him.

The suit spoke volumes and added class to his sexy physique. She loved a man in a suit and Thomas, as she remembered, never failed when it came to dazzling her with is attire.

She looked around at the many eyes that landed on her, the new face around the table. Looks of confusion stared back at her from those who had not yet been made aware that she was a new hire.

"Let me start by welcoming the newest member of our staff, Karen Jacobs. She'll be replacing Anita while she's on maternity leave. Karen will be in the office Wednesday through Friday each week, so plan your scheduling with her accordingly. Let's all make her feel welcomed."

Everyone clapped as Karen made eye contact with each person sitting around the large table. She wanted to do an initial assessment of who she would encounter each day.

"Now, I want each of you to introduce yourself to Karen and let her know what your role is here in the company."

Karen got out her pen and pad and took down information on each person as they gave a history of who they were and what their contribution to the company was.

Thomas had two vice presidents who wielded a lot of power in the company. She made a note to look into both of them a little closer. It had to be someone that high up to have the kind of access to the company's records as the person who was stealing from the retirement fund. She would need to find out who their assistants were and see if she could gather any information they wouldn't have shared at this meeting.

At the end of the meeting, everyone once again welcomed her and some came up to welcome her with a handshake. One of the vice presidents in particular, Carl, held her hand a little longer than she liked and she didn't care for the way he looked at her throughout the meeting as if she were a meaty steak and he was a starving man on a deserted island. He really made her feel uncomfortable when he came to welcome her after everyone else had left.

"Karen, I just wanted to again welcome you to Atwater Industries. You certainly are lovely and quite talented, I hear, when it comes to numbers."

She noted that he said all of this while still holding onto her hand. She had to almost forcibly pry it from his tight grip in order to break away. When she said a quiet thank you and tried to go around him, he blocked her departure.

"So, Thomas tells us that the two of you know each other from childhood. It's funny I never heard him mention you before. Were you not close friends back then?" he asked, inquisitively.

Karen exhaled, smiled and decided to play along since it looked like Carl wasn't going to let her get away without first playing twenty questions.

"We were when we were younger, but I've lived

away from Raleigh for quite a few years and we lost touch when I lived on the west coast. I recently moved back to the area and was planning to get settled in and not work for a bit. I ran into Thomas and he mentioned he needed some help and I was more than happy to lend a hand for a while until his full-time bookkeeper comes back. That's what friends do; they help each other out."

Karen hated how intense his stare was, unnerving her.

"You are Carl, right?" she asked since he was giving her his attention. Him, she would keep an extra eye on.

"Yes, I'm Carl Warner and you'll be seeing me around your office a lot. Anita did all of the bookkeeping, but I always do double and triple checking on them as one of the vice presidents. Maybe you and I should schedule some time to talk more about how we will be working closely together and perhaps I can answer any additional questions you may have about the job and the company. Believe me when I tell you that I am your man for anything you may need."

Karen didn't miss the extra emphasis he placed on the word, 'anything', again causing her radar to go crazy.

"I may take you up on that Carl," she said openly while inside feeling hesitant. Carl, it seems, was the epitome of the word creep.

"Perhaps over lunch one day soon?" he asked,

jumping at the opportunity.

The way he spoke up quickly made her feel dirty. She was getting the feeling that lunch was not what he had on his mind. She watched as he looked at her slowly up and down, spending a little more time on her breasts, even though she knew she was professionally dressed with very little skin showing in that area.

"Sure, we can do that. Why don't you tell me who your assistant is and I'll schedule something with her?"

"Well my assistant is Sheila Donaldson, but you can just deal directly with me with this. I'll stop by perhaps tomorrow and we can talk about lunch then."

He dragged out the word lunch, which was not lost on her. She knew he was definitely one to watch. It was obvious he was the office pervert. She would keep him on her radar and have her office do a more in-depth check on him.

"That will be fine."

Karen needed to get out of the room and away from him. Besides, his cologne would soon turn her to stone if she didn't get away from him. It was a rancid smell and she needed fresh air.

"It was nice to meet you Carl. I will talk to you tomorrow then."

As she exited the conference room, she heard him utter to himself, '*yes you will.*'

8

The workday was moving by fast and when Karen looked up, it was lunch time and then soon after, with her head buried in books again, the rest of the afternoon had gotten away from her. She'd had so much to read up on regarding how Thomas liked the books kept and on the software he used to have everything entered and tracked and time got away from her.

She noticed that though everything was password protected, they were passwords that were easily deciphered by anyone who was close to him. She needed to remember to remind him to change his password and change it more often. She also noticed that the written copies of his financial reports and bookkeeping records were kept in a safe in his office that any child could figure out how to get into. He probably thought that locking the safe and his office when he wasn't in would be enough because he was the company president and people's comings and goings into his office would be monitored. He probably thought everything in his office was safe. She knew that wasn't the case if the person stealing was someone very close to him. She looked up when she heard a sound to again see Thomas standing in her doorway.

"Hi. I wanted to come by and see how your first day was going. I hope we didn't overwhelm you with too much information," he stated.

"Not at all. It's been a good day. Most of it has been spent getting to know some of the key people. I've set up some meetings for tomorrow and Friday to talk one on one with some of them. I'm looking to begin next week by diving into more of the financial records. I didn't realize how much I missed numbers until today. I thought I needed a break and that I was burning out from working so hard for so many years, but that's not the case at all. I'm looking forward to getting off and running with the job. You know me, numbers are my life!" she said excitedly.

She realized she'd caught him by surprise by her excitement because his laugh was so jovial, it brightened up the whole room.

"I'm glad to hear that. It's the end of the day. Are you about to leave yet?" he asked.

"I just noticed how late it was. I guess I was so immersed in work, I let the time get away from me. I need to get out of here and get to the market to grab stuff for dinner."

Thomas couldn't help that he was staring at her. Even in a plain black business suit and white shirt, she was just down right sexy. He knew that had not escaped several of the men around the office. A few made mention in passing at how beautiful she was. He didn't know if he would be crossing a line he shouldn't, but he wanted to spend some time with her. He wasn't sure how open she would be to that given the history they shared, but he was a go-getter if nothing else.

"Say, Karen, would I be overstepping any boundaries if I asked you if you'd like to have dinner with me? You mentioned not having anything for dinner already at home and I haven't eaten either. I thought I'd get me something to eat and if you'd like, I'd love for you to join me."

She could tell he was nervous about asking her and as much as she should say no, she couldn't resist spending a little more time with him, innocently. Besides, she needed to get more information from him so having dinner would be a good cover for doing so.

"That would be nice Thomas, thank you. Let me just stop in the ladies room to freshen up a bit and if you let me know where you'd like to eat, I'll meet you there."

Thomas picked a restaurant, gave her the name and directions and told her he would go ahead and get a table and to just ask for him when she arrived. They agree to meet at seven. Before he walked out Karen had to inquire about his leaving the office already and it was just after six. The Thomas she knew always worked into the wee hours of the night.

"Thomas, it's just after six and you are leaving the office. This is way different from the Thomas I remember," she said shocked.

He turned to face her and spoke softly.

"I'm not the same Thomas you knew back then. The fun and full of life Thomas is still here, but the workaholic Thomas was put to rest. I don't value being in the office all night long or on weekends. I spent years building this company up and hiring just the right people so that I wouldn't have to work as long or as hard as I did in the beginning. I like to be out of here before eight o'clock each night and I even have days where I work at home. Not many, but I've done it a few times. Fancy that, huh?" he said smiling.

Karen smiled back, liking this new Thomas. She wished this was the Thomas she'd had years ago. This is what she wanted back then. It was okay to focus on work, but there were things much more important than that. She believed that, but the idea seemed miniscule right now. As the years went by, she often wished she had not given him an ultimatum and went with her heart instead of her head. Life could have been different for them.

"Yeah, who would have thought?" she replied. Just for good measure she added, "I like this new Thomas. He seems a lot more relaxed."

"That's me. I'm old, relaxed Thomas," he replied

and smiled.

"That's a good thing," she said and meant it.

"I'm going to head out to get us a table and I'll see you about seven."

Karen nodded, not wanting to say anything else. She needed him to leave so that she could once again, exhale. His nearness was playing tricks on her mind and her body and knowing that he wasn't the workaholic that she'd known and that he'd learned to appreciate life more had her feeling all melancholy and that wasn't a good thing.

**

Dinner with Karen was very enjoyable. Thomas was glad they were able to reminisce about old times without any tension or mentioning of what happened to end the relationship they shared. He listened as she shared with him a more in-depth look into her life that he'd missed out on.

She spoke about her friend Lacey who he remembered very clearly. They were closer than two sisters could possibly be. She told him that Lacey was still married and had two small boys. He decided to not ask her why she never married or had any children. If she wanted to share that, he would listen, but he didn't want to pry too far into her personal life. They even talked business. Karen wanted him to give her his impression of those closest to him at the company so that she could learn them even better. He settled in and went down the list of those who worked for him.

Karen paid very close attention when Thomas gave a rundown on Carl. It appeared to be well known that Carl was the office flirt. Thomas mentioned that a few times, he had to talk to Carl about how uncomfortable he made some of the females on the staff feel. He told her he had not heard any real complaints and assumed the women learned how to just deal with Carl by putting him in his place if need be. She could tell by the extra attention he wanted to give her that she would probably have to do that with him much sooner than later herself.

She also asked him a little about the security around the financial records. She knew that the accounting office kept good track of everything financial with the company and with Thomas having two chief financial officers besides himself, he knew that the company was pretty stable financially. As for the files the bookkeeper was responsible for, Thomas had been impressed with the job Anita had been doing over the years. He admitted he divided the financial responsibilities between himself, Carl and the other financial officer, Brad. He trusted them without any doubt and he trusted the work they did to help him build a successful business. She had some doubts about that and tonight she would send information to her team to have them get more information on both men and she'd take it from there. In the meantime, she'd do a little snooping around where she could to see what she could find.

"So, tell me, how is your family? Are your aunt and uncle still living and what about your mother?"

"Yes, they are all doing fine," he said.

"Wonderful!"

"Yeah. My aunt and uncle live in Florida now. They have both retired and are living the perfect life. I make sure I go visit them as often as I can. I will probably go down in a few weeks just to get away for a bit and it's my aunt's birthday so I'm planning on surprising her. My mother still lives in the Bahamas and has been married about three now. They are very happy and he seems like a good guy"

"I'm glad to hear your mother is doing so well. That's great."

There was silence before he continued on and Karen could tell he was struggling with whatever he was going to say next.

"You know I never found my father. Even when I had the money to do so, I had someone looking into it for a while and then I decided to leave it alone. You know I use to think I was missing something by not having him around, when actually I didn't. I don't have any anger or hatred because according to my mother, he would not have known about me so I can't blame him for not being around. She didn't find out she was pregnant until he had already left to return to his life, which you already know about. She told me one day she suspected that he was probably married at the time and that what they had was more of an island fling that produced me. I let it go and realized my uncle did everything with and for me that any father would do and I was blessed to have him. What about you Karen? Are you close to your family, especially after your mother passed? I was sorry to hear about that, by the way. I actually didn't hear about it until months after she had passed. My aunt thought I knew about it or that someone had told me when I was living in New York. Once when I had come back to town to visit, she was the one who told me that you had moved out of town after your mother passed and all she knew was that it was someplace on the west coast."

"Thank you for that Thomas. My mother died peacefully. She had suffered with cancer for a long time and in the end, all I could do was keep her comfortable with medication. One morning when I went to check on her, she had slipped away during the night. Other than Lacey, she was my only real connection to the area, so moving was easy and it was something I needed to do."

"I understand and I'm glad to know you're doing so well. I see the time is really getting late now and we both need to be at the office early in the morning."

Again, time had gotten away from her and this time because she was enjoying his company. For a little while, she was able to forget he was the target of her investigation.

"Thank you for dinner. It's nice to be able to sit down and talk to you. It's the one thing I missed most when we broke up. You were the one person besides Lacey that I could talk to," Karen admitted.

"I've missed talking to you as well. We did have some great talks."

They were looking at each other, neither breaking the stare as the air around them became electric. Karen could feel it and she knew Thomas could as well. This wasn't good and she agreed that it was time to leave.

"Well, the bed calls," she said and then she was embarrassed when she thought about her words. It was too late to take them back now that she'd said them.

Thomas caught what she'd said as well. Rather than make her feel uncomfortable about the statement, he just smiled as he stood for them to leave. He walked over to her to slide her chair out and help her up.

"It's okay. I know what you meant. I'm nervous around you too," he said.

Karen exhaled and felt a lot better. She wasn't in this nervous game alone.

"Thanks again for dinner and for the job. Today was so busy, time went by. I think this will also give me some insight into starting my own company."

"If you need any help with that, let me know."

She turned to him.

"You'll be the first I'll come to for help since I see how successful you have been starting yours."

Thomas walked her out to her car and waited until she pulled off into traffic before getting in his own car.

He sat outside of the restaurant well after Karen had gotten in her car and driven away. It was now real to him and even if he never tells her, he knew he was still in love with her. He could fight it if he wanted to, but years apart didn't lessen his feelings for her. She had been working for him for one day and he was already having a hard time controlling his feelings about her. He knew he was treading in dangerous territory with his feelings.

When Karen mentioned at dinner that her bed was calling her, all he could think of was their sweaty bodies, grinding on that said bed while he did unspeakable things to her body; things he wanted to do again and again. That was the reason why he got up right after her comment. He feared he would do something stupid like ask her to come home with him. Thomas was ready to pick right up and start a new relationship with her, but he knew, even if she didn't say so, the hurt he'd caused her was still there. Karen was more mature now and it appeared that the past was in the past for them, but he also knew that women were very emotional. He wasn't sure that she was able to just forgive and forget, especially if he tried to get close to her again. He wanted her in the worst way and he knew he had to bide his time to let her see who he was and if he was worth her giving him another chance. She was back and he already knew he didn't want to let her go again.

9

It was week two for Karen at Atwater Industries and things were going well. The FBI had provided her with follow-up information on other company employees and she'd narrowed the list down to who could be involved in the theft. She had also been keeping an eye on those closest to Thomas and realized Carl Warren was sleazy enough to undercut Thomas and steal from him and now she had to prove it. There wasn't anything she liked about him and he gave her good reason to not like him.

Carl, though married, was involved in an affair with one of the women, Liza, from the accounting office. How convenient was that, she thought, that he would be involved with someone who deals with the company's finances every day and who could potentially help him if he were the one stealing. She'd find a way to befriend Liza and see if she could get any information from her.

Carl Warner didn't like new people at all, she discovered with her interactions with him. He especially didn't like new people who appeared to be sucking up to the company president. He knew that she and Thomas had been friends back in the day, but he wondered what kind of friends they were and it bothered him that he couldn't get a handle on that information.

Carl had mentioned in passing one day that he'd noticed on several occasions strange looks she and Thomas gave each other. He told her, if he didn't know any better, he would think that they had something going on.

She walked past his office and decided to stop by.

"Hey, Carl. Sheila said it was okay to stop in and say hello. I have a few minutes before a meeting and I was walking around and seeing how things operate around here."

She watched as he stood and came around his desk to greet her. He came close, too close, causing her to step back a little. He was definitely a space invader, someone who had not respect for another person's personal space.

"I'm glad you stopped by. We never did get a chance to have lunch so that I can give you my perspective on how things work around here. Perhaps we can do that soon?"

Karen knew that at first his invitation to lunch was more about personal, unsavory reasons, but now she suspected he was digging for information, especially since he believed there was more to her friendship with Thomas than just friendship.

"We can do that. I do have some questions for you that would help me in my daily work, so let's make that lunch happen real soon. I better get to my meeting. Let me know about lunch and I'll be there," she said, turning to leave.

"I'll do that," Carl said to her back as she left. He gave her the creeps and she felt like she needed to take a hot shower after every interaction with him.

Carl went back to his desk and sat down. There was something about Karen that he didn't like yet he couldn't put his finger on what it was. He had a feeling it wasn't something good and delicious though those are two words he used to describe her. He'd like to get close to her, but he had a feeling she wasn't an airhead like some of the other women around the company and he'd be asking for trouble if he made a play for her. That would be disappointing because he was instantly attracted to the beauty from the first day she started working for them.

He had tried, unsuccessfully to flirt with her, trying to use his power and prestige within the company to win her over, but she was a hard cookie to crack. He decided to let it go which was why he hadn't brought up lunch again with her. When she took it upon herself to visit him today, he figured why not give lunch another try. He doubted if he would get her into bed like he wanted, but he'd been turned down by plenty of women before and besides, Liza was allowing him to smack it, flip it and rub it up, down and all around whenever he wanted. She was a firecracker in the sack, much different than his killjoy of a wife. He smiled when he realized soon, he wouldn't have to worry about that ball and chain anymore. He had big plans that included Liza, but not his wife.

Carl's plan was coming to an end soon and he would say so long to working for the company and finally living the life of luxury he's always wanted to live. He had to admit, he was pretty well off thanks to the very profitable Atwater Industries. His money hungry wife was sucking up all of his money with her frivolous spending. He smiled knowing that soon, he would no longer care what she did. He'd be gone, taking whatever money he had left and he would disappear from her life forever. He and Liza would be happy and rich, far away from working every day. He snickered when he thought about his plan for his future.

For now, he was in the clear. It appeared no one knew what he and Liza had been up to and if they could keep it up just a little longer, they would be singing all the way to the bank. He needed to keep an eye on the new bookkeeper though. He could tell she was bright and intelligent and he had to be sure she didn't come across anything that would lead her to discover and report what he had been doing. If she were humping the boss, he knew where her loyalty would lie and he couldn't have that. He'd come too far in his plan to let anyone deter him and he would take care of anyone that got in his way. He had spent years cooking up this scheme and now that he was close to the end, nothing and no one would get in his way. Definitely not some new, nosey bookkeeper.

**

It was late in the day, the last day of the week and Thomas was thankful it was the weekend. He was planning to do some work preparing for the fundraiser he would be taking part in. His lunch meeting with Phil had not yet been rescheduled, but he had a few more community partnerships that he was involved in and all involved working with youth programs. He would get to meet some of the youth this weekend and he looked forward to that. He also looked forward to getting a few days' reprieve from running into Karen every day. This week, she had actually come into the office all five days since there were plans in place for an expansion of the company and she'd been instrumental in the ideas she'd offered up at the meetings. He was appreciative of her help as a bookkeeper, but he was finding it harder and harder, literally, each day to resist finding a reason to be near her or speak to her.

Thomas loved how dedicated she was to her work and realized she had even worked a little over a few days and this was only her second week with the company. She was determined to not let anything slip when it came to her job. Stopping by her office every day to see what she was wearing was starting to become the norm for him.

Today, she wore a fire red dress with high red heeled shoes that made her legs look like they went on forever. His desire for her grew with each passing day and he had no doubt that she'd caught him several times ogling her, but he couldn't help it because her presence was becoming intoxicating. He wasn't sure how much longer he would be able to resist asking her to dinner or a movie or anything just to be around her more and on a personal level. He wanted anything she would be willing to offer as long as he had a chance to spend some time with her. It wasn't until he'd seen her again that he realized how much he had missed her over the years. He loved everything about her from her dedication to the job to her lovely smile to the way she dealt with the staff and then on top of that, she showed no ill-will toward him for their past and he respected that about her.

Thomas gathered what he needed from his office before heading out. He noticed even more of a change in himself and those around him mentioned it a time or two. He didn't want to admit it was due to Karen's presence back in his life because he hadn't told anyone about their history, though Carl had begun asking him a lot of questions. He had a feeling Carl was either picking up on a vibe between him and Karen or Carl, like so many times in the past, was trying to make a play for her and wanted to be sure they weren't in competition. Being married didn't stop Carl from seeking out other women and one thing he knew for sure about Karen and that was she would never get involved with a married man. Still he would need to be careful around Carl when he encountered Karen to keep down any gossip Carl might spread.

He wasn't too keen on his financial officer and lately, he'd found that Carl may be up to some illegal dealings, but he had no proof. He was planning to hire an investigator to look into it quietly. Carl had come highly recommended and with several degrees under his belt, he worked his way into the position he now held, but something was off and Thomas needed to find out what. For now, he turned his focus back to Karen and wondered how much longer he'd be able to resist asking her out.

10

Karen had plans to spend her weekend doing more checking into Carl and Liza. Carl had been married for fifteen years and though the marriage seemed happy to the outside world, Karen had found they weren't happy at all.

Carl made lots of money while his wife enjoyed spending it as fast as he made it. Right before money started disappearing at Atwater, he had started an office affair with Liza that was still going on. A few people knew of it, but most either didn't care or didn't say anything for fear it would cost them a job. She didn't know if Thomas knew about it, but with the way gossip spread around the office, he'd have to be living on a deserted island to at least not hear the rumors.

Liza didn't have any family in the area. She had gone to college in the North Carolina area and when she graduated with a degree in accounting, she stayed when she accepted a job at Atwater following an internship that had gone extremely well. Karen was sure it was because her internship was served working directly for Carl and that's probably when the affair started. Carl was a fast talker and played himself and his financial status up and Liza was just feeble minded enough to fall for it. Earlier in the week, she saw Carl hand something to Liza looking around to be sure no one was looking. Though the two of them were working hard to be discreet, she noticed obvious signs of flirting and public displays of affection that shouldn't be for others in the office to see.

Karen quickly realized in her short time at the company that the target of her investigation should be Carl and Liza and her next game plan was to get closer to Liza. She had to find out what she knew and how deeply involved she was.

Monday would be a key day for her since she was having an in-person briefing with the local FBI office to go over she was able to find out so far. She knew they wanted her focus on Thomas, but she was expanding her investigation and would inform them as soon as she had more concrete information to share. It was the weekend and for now, she wanted to take her mind off of work and relax around the house. She wanted to take a day or two and be free from any work-related tasks. While preparing to load clothes in the washing machine, her phone rang. She looked at the number and didn't recognize it. She knew it had to be someone from her job or another local, maybe a wrong number.

"Hello?"

"Hello, Karen. I hope I didn't catch you at a bad time."

It was Thomas. Just hearing his deep, low and seductive voice did things to her body. It somehow remembered the sound of his voice and how he could pleasure it.

"Hi. This is a surprise. Is there a work problem or is something wrong?" she asked, hoping it wasn't and secretly desiring a personal reason for the call.

She noticed the hesitation before he responded.

"No, everything is fine with work. I was actually calling for a more personal reason and I hope that's okay."

She had hoped so.

"Sure."

"I was wondering if you were free for a late lunch or early dinner tonight with me. I understand if you say no. I have been walking around my house all morning thinking about you and wondering if I'd be out of line asking you out considering our history or at least how that history ended. I promise I did everything to take my mind off of you and tried hard to not put you in an uncomfortable position and I'm hoping I'm not putting my foot in my mouth. I want to spend some time with you where we aren't talking about work."

Thomas waited for what seemed an eternity for her to speak.

Karen smiled now that she knew she wasn't the

only one struggling with her feelings and everything in her said to just say no. She ignored that feeling.

"I'd love to. Lunch or an early dinner would be fine."

He felt hopeful.

"Great. I'll pick you up at your house around five and thanks for saying yes."

"I look forward to it," she acknowledged before hanging up.

After ending the call, Karen caught herself smiling and moving around the house feeling like she wanted to dance. In the back of her mind, she knew she should have said no and kept things between she and Thomas about work, but she was finding it very hard to resist wanting to be with him. She probably should not have taken the assignment, but her plan from the start was to prove he wasn't guilty of anything and she planned to still do that. She also knew she wanted him with a fierceness that wouldn't go away. Wasn't she entitled to some happiness?

**

Dinner was the best idea Thomas had come up with in a long while. He and Karen were having a great time as if time had stood still for them and they were picking up where things were back then, when they were happy and in love. They laughed about some funny television shows and she even told him some very funny stories about her godsons. Thomas could tell she longed for children of her own and he was sorry that they'd never had any together. Even though she didn't say she would give dating him again a try, that's what he wanted, but he would take things very slow.

"You are so beautiful," he said glancing at her across the table. They were at a restaurant on the outskirts of town so that she would feel comfortable being out with him without any prying eyes from people at the office.

Karen blushed, delighted by his compliment.

"Thank you."

Thomas watched as she first looked away and then captured his eyes again and what he saw looking back at him was how he was feeling about her; she wanted him, too. He remembered all of her looks and he could never mistake her look of want and her passionate look of need. Just as he had never gotten over her, it was apparent she had never gotten over him either. They were near the end of dinner and he wanted to draw the time out tonight so that they could spend time beyond the restaurant.

"Listen, there is a carnival the next county over. I was wondering if you'd like to go, maybe ride a few rides? Eat some cotton candy? I don't want the night to end yet," he said.

"That sounds like fun. Let's do it."

They talked as they drove to the carnival. Karen wished she could be honest about her life in recent years as an agent, but she knew she had to continue playing the role. She was confusing her own self trying to keep up the façade and not let anything slip. She rehearsed in her mind over and over again the story of her life since they parted that was created for her specifically for this case.

"So, how was Seattle? I actually had business dealings there a few times and since we ran in the same circles, I was surprised to never run into you while I was there on business."

No sweat and no need to panic, she thought. Seattle is a large place.

"I loved it, but it was cold and rainy and I was over both. I find that I missed the warm southern climate and when I decided to take a break, this was the first place I thought of coming to."

Thomas nodded and pulled into a parking spot. He would continue the conversation later while they walked around. For now, he wanted to have fun.

The carnival was just the type of evening Karen needed. She hadn't had this much fun in years. They had ridden the rollercoaster, driven bumper cars, ate more snack food than should be legally allowed and she didn't hesitate when Thomas reached out and entwined their fingers together as they walked, talked and laughed. She missed this and she missed Thomas.

It was getting late and they decided to make the Ferris wheel their last ride of the night. Karen remembered when they dated years ago, they loved the Ferris wheel. They would get in it, kiss and get carried away until they had to get off to find a bed. After all, isn't that what couples got on it for?

She could tell when she was seated next to Thomas that he was thinking the same thoughts that she was. He was also recalling the many moments they'd had on a Ferris wheel. Without thinking and as the wheel reached the top, she turned towards Thomas and as their eyes met and like in their past, no words were needed as they met in the middle. The moment was reminiscent of a time when they enjoyed each other the way they had today.

Karen's eyes grew glassy with tears pooling in them at the thought that she longed to be with him like this again and she was about to get that chance. She watched as Thomas reached out to stroke her cheek and his lips came down on hers in a tender, yet powerful kiss full of possibilities. She swooned as he drank from her mouth and being an equal partner in the kiss, she offered her mouth up to him, letting him know she was with him all the way. She groaned into his mouth and moved even closer needing to feel more than just his lips. Wrapping her arms around Thomas' neck, she went willingly into his arms as he drew her closer, flush against his chest where she thought that he could feel his heart beating rapidly in his chest. He was having an uncontrollable reaction that matched hers. If it were not for the bar that held them down in their seats, she knew he would have pulled her into his lap.

Thomas was ready to burst. This was his Karen and he had her back in his arms in a way that he thought he'd only get this again in his dreams. This was no dream. She was real and there was no way he could think up a kiss this good. Moving apart when the ride moved again, both struggled to catch their breath. Nothing had ever felt so right and being here with Karen is how their life was supposed to be. Thomas' enthusiasm had him plunging back into her mouth like a starving man and he didn't miss that Karen returned the kiss with just as much fervor. They knew the kiss had to end when they both needed to breathe and the ride had come to a stop for them to exit. They were embarrassed when they opened their eyes and stared into the faces of the people who were waiting to get in the ride next. Laughing they exited the ride, feeling like two teenagers caught fooling around.

They laughed about getting caught all the way back to Karen's house. Thomas loved that he could make her laugh and smile again. When he pulled up in the driveway, neither moved to get out. He wanted to come in, but he needed her to do the inviting. It was clear what it meant if they stepped out of the car and entered the house together. His gaze raked all over her as they sat in silence. Karen was thinking and he gave her time to do it. He could tell she'd made a decision about what was next when she looked over at him and smiled. Her next words weren't a question, but a statement.

"I want you to come in, Thomas," she said on a breathy whisper.

He didn't respond, but instead turned off the car, got out and went around to help her out. They entered the house through the garage and the minute they were inside with the door locked, they were all over each other. This time there was no pretense in waiting for who would initiate the kiss. Karen leaned up, grasped Thomas by the back of his neck and drew their lips together in a kiss that left no doubt about what was in store. She went at his lips almost attacking them. She felt Thomas relax as he allowed her to set the pace and control the moment.

This is the kind of deep-rooted passion Thomas has needed since she came back into his life. This is what he missed about having her.

"I want to make love to you," he said as he broke the kiss to be sure she was clear on his intent. He wanted to give her time to say no and he'd stop. He stood staring down at her waiting for a sign of whether he should proceed in that direction. Karen used her hands to roam from his chest down to the belt that secured his pants. She never broke the intense stare they shared as she unbuckled his belt, lowered his zipper and slipped her hand inside to stroke his long, thick and veiny length. The feel of her hand on him had his breaths coming out deep and harsh.

Thomas was struggling to breathe with the way her hand felt sliding up and down his hardness. If he thought he needed a verbal response from Karen, he was wrong because she had other ideas in mind. While she continued driving him crazy with her hand and possessively kissing him, he unbuttoned her shirt to reveal her perfect globes encased in a sky blue demi bra, giving him a teasing view. He pulled the shirt from her arms, briefly removing her hand from his pants. She was about to fuss with him for doing so until he reached for her hand and placed it back where they both wanted it, back down the front of his pants. They were frenzy for each other as things started moving at lightning speed.

Finally removing his shirt, Thomas reached to remove her slacks and even with her hand still diligently stroking him, he tugged down his own pants pulling his boxers down and off along with them. Before tossing them to the side, he reached in his pocket for protection. He walked them slowly backward to the nearest sofa where he sat down with her straddling his lap. He quickly dispersed with her barely their panties by pulling on the thin strips at the side of her hips that were held together by a bow. Releasing it, they fell away and his eyes settled on the area between her legs that was already glistening as the little bit of light in the room showed the wetness that had gathered there. He didn't plan to make her wait too long since he knew he wouldn't last much longer either. He'd waited too long to have her again and waiting would prolong the misery for them both.

Thomas took her mouth in another kiss while he struggled to get the condom on. When it was secure, he opened her legs wider and positioned himself at her opening. Not waiting another minute, he entered her thrusting upward over and over again, snatching the air from their lungs the moment was so powerful. He watched as Karen threw her head back and rode him setting a pace that was not slow or patterned. It was wild with reckless abandonment.

Karen was in another world where nothing existed except for the feel of Thomas hard and strong surging in and out of her at a pace that had her begging for more and more. Each time Thomas lunged up into her, she pushed down on him and the friction was sending her to another plateau. She was tumbling quickly back down to earth when Thomas screamed her name.

"Karen, baby, I'm there!"

"I'm with you, Thomas. Come on, sweetie, I'm right with you," Karen said as her orgasm crashed into her. It went on and on as she increased the speed of her downward plunges on to him as she felt him grab her hips tighter and rode out his own orgasm screaming through his release right into her chest.

When their breathing finally slowed down to a normal pace, Thomas leaned back, bringing Karen with him and they stayed in that position with neither wanting to separate. It had taken them too long to get back to this place to move away from each other now.

11

A full month on the job and Karen felt herself falling into a routine that involved working on the investigation during the day and working on what she and Thomas were developing together at night. In the midst of it all, she spent time wrestling with what she was doing. She had arrived in town to solve a case and not get involved with Thomas again, but she couldn't avoid being with him even if she wanted to. The pull to him was as it was when they were younger and had just met. It was almost as if time had actually stopped and took them back to a time where they never went their separate ways.

The night before, she laid awake in his arms while he slept and she wondered how bad the situation would get if those who sent here to Raleigh to do a job discovered that she was once again falling in love with Thomas, a man who wasn't just anyone, but the man she was sent to investigate and according to the FBI, should be locked up for stealing from his own company. Now more than ever, she needed to get the case wrapped up so that the weight of her deceit would lessen. She wasn't just lying to Thomas, she was also lying to the FBI by not telling them that she was doing more than investigating or that she was now going in a new direction that led away from Thomas. Now in the office, she had to put thoughts of her nights with Thomas on the back burner and concentrate on the case.

A lot had been going on at Atwater and she knew beyond any doubt that Carl was in fact the embezzler. Over the past week, she had finally been able to befriend Liza like her plan called for. In one of their girl talks, Liza had let it slip that Carl was going to leave his wife and they were going to move away together to live a life of luxury. Karen didn't think Liza was supposed to tell her that, but she also knew Liza was excited to have a friend at work. Liza wasn't at all secretive about her affair with Carl and Karen had discovered that Liza actually had the combination to the safe in Carl's office. If she was ever going to find out what Carl kept there, she had to find a way to talk Liza into giving her the combination without blowing her cover.

On Friday, she'd walked in on Carl going through the items in his safe and when he noticed her standing at his door, he nervously closed it and stuttered out his words and she knew he was covering up something. Lucky for her, he hadn't shut it before she got a glimpse of what looked like red ledgers. Karen remembered from her files about the case that the bookkeeper she replaced mentioned the red ledgers that Thomas usually kept were what she thought she was looking at.

Anita had gone into the accounting office and saw the ledger sticking out from a drawer at Liza's desk and knew that it supposed to be in Thomas' safe. She knew it couldn't be Carl's because the only red ledgers where Thomas'. Everyone else used black or blue ledgers and Thomas was quite adamant about no one else using red. She had picked it up, leaving Liza a note reminding her to always replace the ledgers when not entering information in them. The note said she would put this one back for her since she was about to leave for the day. Anita quickly skimmed through the ledger to see what the new entries were that Liza must have entered and she became confused. What she saw was different than what she remembered. She made a note to check it later when she got side tracked with a few phone calls and a trip to the copy room on another floor.

Later, when Anita returned, she saw that things on her desk had been moved around and the ledger that she'd placed under a lot of files on her desk was now sitting on top, something she never did. Someone had moved it. She opened it and her first thought was that this was a different ledger than the one she looked at before going to the copy room. The one she looked at the second time had information and figures that matched what she knew to be correct. She found it odd and knew that something strange was going on.

As her suspicions grew, weeks later, the FBI had been brought in on the case. From the little she'd read in the ledger, she knew those funds were going into an account that wasn't any of Thomas' accounts that were known to her. She had initially suspected Thomas because he was back in his office by the time she returned from the copy room and he came right out and asked her about the ledger, saying he needed it. She couldn't think of who else could have slipped up and exchanged the ledgers so quickly since her office was right outside of his and she hadn't been gone that long. She brought it to his attention and dismissed it.

Karen had a plan already in place. She had secured a mini camera and had placed it in Carl's office in a position to record the next time he opened his safe. She needed the combination to see what was inside and either she got it from Liza who she had a feeling knew it and was heavily involved or she waited to see what the camera would show. For now, she would wait.

As luck would have it, earlier in the day, she had walked by Carl's office while his assistant was away from her desk and she overheard Liza and Carl talking behind the closed office door. She stood to the side and listened as Carl talked about the two of them soon having more money than they could have ever dreamed of and before anyone found out they would be long gone. Liza then mentioned how it all could have been blown to hell if she wasn't able to get that ledger back before Anita had discovered she'd picked up the wrong one. He told her to keep a closer eye on the ledger and always remember to put it back in his safe so that it wouldn't get mixed up with Thomas' until they were ready to execute their plan.

For the rest of that day, Karen watched Carl and Liza and took note of everything they did. It wasn't until the close of the day that she realized Carl had gone into his safe and hopefully the recorder she had set up had recorded the combination. She waited around faking additional work she had to get done after most of the staff had left. Thinking everyone had gone, she walked toward the main office suites toward Carl's office and noticed the light was on in Thomas' office at the far end of the hall. Not wanting to be caught by him, she walked ahead to his office to try to get an idea of how long he'd be hanging around. As she walked, the cell phone in her hand buzzed and looking down at it, it was Thomas texting her, asking if she was still in the office. She sent a text back acknowledging that she was and he asked her to stop up. To not make it obvious that she was already near his office, she waited a few minutes before walking through his office door to make it seem as if she'd come up from her own office.

"You called," Karen said seductively, placing her hands on her shapely hips and turned on the charm. She may be faking the reason why she was working for him, but there was nothing fake about her growing feelings for him.

Thomas looked up and the look in Karen's eyes told him everything he needed to know. He was in love with her and she looked heavenly standing in the doorway. Seeing her, he literally rose to the occasion in more ways than one.

"I sure did. Did you see anyone else in the office on your way here?" Thomas asked with a devious tone.

"No one, but you and little ol' me," she replied cunningly.

"Well, since we're all alone and I can't seem to get you off of my mind, I was wondering if you could check me out to see if I may have a fever. I seem to be a little hot," he said loosening his tie and faking feeling for a heated temperate across his forehead with the back of his hand.

Karen knew that look and knew what he had in mind.

"Well, I guess I can do that since bookkeeping isn't my only skill."

Thomas moaned as she came closer.

"Wow, do tell," he said moving past her to close and lock his office door before pulling her with him over to his office chair where he sat down, pulling her down onto his lap in the perfect position for her to feel how much he'd been thinking about her and how badly he wanted her.

Nuzzling her neck while caressing her legs, Thomas said, "I'd love to hear all about these other skills you have."

"I'll show you mine if you show me yours."

Thomas didn't need more of an invitation than the one she just gave him. He turned around in his chair, lifted Karen up and placed her on the top of his desk, right at the edge.

Karen's lips parted on a gasp as she realized his intent. Multi-tasking, she watched Thomas loosen his tie, unbutton his shirt and spread her legs open in front of his face, all while never taking his eyes off of hers.

"I'll go first," he said.

"You don't play fair. I was about to display my skills first," she said, feeling her body already humming.

"Plenty of time for that sweetheart," he said and without any pretense, Thomas moved forward placing his head between her legs and stroked the seam of her panties with his tongue, causing moisture to pool at her center.

"Ahh," she said throwing her head back.

"Mmm, what have you been thinking about? You're so wet."

He then slowly licked her again and this time, Karen placed one of her hands on his head, making sure he knew she liked what he was doing to her.

She tried to concentrate on his question, but her body would only allow her to focus on his magical tongue. She felt lightheaded, like she had been drugged. Moving her hips in tandem with his tongue, she told him first with her body that it was him she had been thinking about and then she added the words.

"You," she whispered. "I've been thinking about you."

Thomas needed more as he moved her panties to the side and placed his tongued directly on her wetness and without showing any mercy, he gave her what she needed and what he wanted. Her taste was mesmerizing. He licked and lapped at her all while enjoying the mewing sounds of enjoyment coming from her mouth. Her sounds ignited a fire so intense, he knew any moment he would burst into flames from the magnitude of how much he wanted her. Never in his wildest dreams did he ever imagine he'd be able to enjoy her this way again. The gods were definitely in is corner.

Karen's world was spinning as the feel of Thomas' lips and tongue drove her mad. The impact of a mind-numbing, sizzling, toe-curling orgasm made its way through her body and she exploded. She thrashed about thankful that Thomas was holding her in place as her body climbed and climbed the mountain of neve-rending pleasure, the likes of anything she ever thought she could experience. This was a feeling she had no doubt she would only be able to experience with Thomas.

"That was incredible," she said the moment she was able to speak again.

As she slowly opened her eyes, she saw Thomas stand, licking his lips letting her see he enjoyed that sexual meal very much. She watched as he moved away as if they were done and she reached out and pulled him back toward her. Looking at him like she could eat him alive, she made sure to get across her amorous feelings for him and her desire for more. It was time for him to be putty in her hands.

"Oh, no you don't. It's my turn to have my way with you. Why don't you have a seat in your hair," she said, sliding seductively down off of the table onto wobbly legs. She laughed when Thomas had to reach out to steady her.

"Are you sure you can stand?" he asked.

"After what I just experienced, I'm surprised I haven't passed out by now. I'm good on my legs, but you know what? Let's see how good and steady I am on my knees."

Proving her point, Karen kept her eyes locked on Thomas' as she widened his legs now that he was seated and she moved between them. Before he had a chance to question what she was about to do, she reached for his zipper, reached inside and pulled out that part of him that she couldn't stop thinking about. Clearly, him pleasuring her had made him rock hard, solid and ready for her. Thomas was about to speak when with the speed of light, she moved her head, with her eyes still on his, and lowered her lips over the mushroomed head of him. To say the feeling of him hard and silky smooth in her mouth was erotic was an understatement. Adding her hand to the motion, she stroked him up and down while she caressed him first with her tongue and then taking more of him in, she worked her lips down his hard length. Internally, she smiled, since her lips were busy, at the sight of Thomas enjoying her loving him this way. She heard him moan and the moment she heard him growl, she increased the pace of her actions.

Thomas' head was about to spin off of his shoulders. He couldn't see straight or hear anything; all he could do was feel and what he was feeling was sheer exuberance and a craving to let go and just let his entire body go limp. He had no energy as Karen's mouth worked him again and again. He felt her tongue as it lapped at him up, down, around while his legs began to tremble. He wanted to hold them still, but the mutual assault of her tongue and lips drove him mad as waves of heat flooded through him. He felt the makings of powerful orgasm as he moved his hips in tandem with the rhythm her love making had set for him. No longer capable of holding on to anymore he tried to move Karen out of the way before he exploded, but when he felt her push back to stay in place and knew what she wanted, he let her have everything as he exploded in her mouth. His body and his world rocked and quaked starting in his feet and making its way to his shaft as he became lost in the sensation of pure sexual bliss.

Karen didn't stop when Thomas exploded because she wanted all of him. She needed him to know that she desired to pleasure him the same way he had always given her his all. She continued until his body went limp in the chair and he struggled to breathe. She felt alive as a post coital haze surrounded them and the intimate moments they'd just shared. This, she knew, was exactly what she had longed for in a relationship and it was what she also missed in the time she was away from him. Case or not, she knew she would always want him.

Thomas leaned forward and pulled Karen into his lap, kissing her like a starving man.

"That was amazing baby," he said, trying to stifle a moan that managed to escape his lips as she took his tongue and made love to it like she had just done to his member. This woman was once again his world.

"You are amazing," she said, leaning down to nuzzle his neck. They sat like that for what seemed an eternity. Love was once again in the air, even if neither of them admitted it.

12

Karen walked into the local FBI office in dark shades and a sweat suit with the jacket pulled up and over her head. Even though the office was out of the way, she had to be sure no one recognized her going into the building. Though she had fallen into a routine of falling in love with Thomas again, she had to remember she was on a case and now she needed to give an update on her findings, which were a step in the right direction, leading her to Carl as the number one suspect and not Thomas. She had to convince her superiors that as for Thomas, they were barking up the wrong tree.

She made her way through security and then toward the private conference room on the third floor where her team was waiting for her and her Director in his office in Washington, D.C., would be on the video tele-conferencing system, patched in to see and speak directly to her. She had already emailed him her updates and now she needed to bring everyone else up to date. Knocking on the door, she entered and took a seat across from the four men waiting for her in the office.

"Hi, Karen."

"Hello," she replied nervously. On her way up in the elevator, she wondered if any of them were clued into the sexual relationship she and Thomas had begun again, now that she was back in Raleigh. She knew that her professionalism would be questioned if anyone found out. Thankfully, if asked about the amount of time they had been spending together over past eight weeks since she'd arrived, she could use the excuse of getting as much information out of him as she could. She knew that she was compromising everything about the case by not keeping their relationship to one based on work, but old feelings had crept back up and she couldn't fight the attraction even if she tried. If asked, she wasn't sure what she'd say because her one and only goal was to clear Thomas of any suspicion.

"Karen, it's good to have you in the office today to give us an update," her Director said.

"Were you able to take a look at the file I sent you?" she asked.

"I did and everyone around the table has also. Is Thomas or anyone else at Atwater Industries aware of your presence as anything other than a new employee?"

"As far as I can tell, no one suspects anything. I think Carl is snooping around and I gave information about him in the file," she said, glad that it seems that her personal relationship with Thomas was still a secret. She had no doubt, if she had been compromised, that would have been the first thing out of her boss' mouth.

"Great and I do have to admit, from the information you've been able to gather so far, it does appear the focus of your investigation is turning from Thomas to Carl. How sure are you about Carl's involvement and are you absolutely sure Thomas isn't aware of what's going on?"

"Sir, I'm one hundred percent sure," she admitted, keeping her professional face on. She needed them to see she was all about business. She watched as he looked through several pages before speaking again.

"What's your next move? We need to get this wrapped up as soon as possible. If what you say is true, Carl may try and skip town soon and we need hard evidence. Do you think you can get that?"

"Yes, sir. I have a plan in place and I should have this wrapped up soon. I'm working on an angle that will involve the woman I told you he's having an affair with. I think she'll be the key to getting the information I need. I'll have this wrapped up soon."

After an hour of going over all of the details in her report, she exhaled when everyone agreed that she should pursue Carl, but also keep looking into Thomas. They didn't want any stones left unturned if there was a chance that more than one person was involved.

"I'm glad to hear things should be wrapping up soon and you'll be happy, I'm sure, when you can return to your life in D.C."

Karen held her composure at the thought of leaving Raleigh again and leaving Thomas. In all of the time they had been spending together secretly for the past eight weeks, she forgot the fact that as soon as the case was over, she would return to her life in Washington; one that did not include Thomas. Though she felt sad inside and her heart rate sped up as worry set in, she kept a straight face. She still had a case to wrap up and she'd have to find a way to deal with Thomas afterwards. She knew the hardest part would be revealing to him that she had joined his company under false pretenses. They were enjoying each other, but she had a feeling that as soon as Thomas found out the truth, they would be over. She would lose him again and this time it really would be her fault.

**

Eight weeks sometimes seemed like a lifetime. For Karen, it wasn't long enough. After leaving the FBI office, she had gone home to shower and change and was now on her way to Thomas' house where he had invited her over for a dinner that, according to him, he would be cooking himself. She smiled on the drive to his house like a woman madly in love. She never thought she could be this happy and every time she thought about Thomas, her heart skipped a happy beat.

This day marked exactly eight weeks since she'd walked into the restaurant and started down her current path. Now that she had him back, she hoped through to the end of this case that they would still find a way to make a relationship work, even through her deceit. She had to work out how she would break the news about the FBI investigation to him where he wouldn't be upset with her. She would start out by telling him that she never suspected him, but she couldn't pass up doing whatever she could to help him. If she did that, she was sure he would understand and listen while she told him everything else. That was how she hoped things would go. She first had to nail Carl and she knew she had to do it soon. The longer this dragged on, the harder it would be for Thomas to understand her keeping her real reason for being at Atwater Industries a secret.

Thomas lived just outside of the Raleigh city limits, something Karen learned from his file. She didn't want him to know she knew anything about his home, so when he described it to her, she reacted as if she didn't already know what the house looked like.

She arrived at Thomas' estate, because it was much more than just a house, and was greeted at the door by a gentleman who escorted her inside, took her personal items and asked for her keys so that he could move her car to one of the garages. He then escorted her into the kitchen where

Thomas was busy going between stirring one pot and chopping up items for a salad. He lit up when he saw her enter and she returned his look of elation.

"Well, hello beautiful. I'm glad you could make it," he said enthusiastically.

Karen ventured all the way into the kitchen and marveled at the sheer size of it. It was more like a kitchen made for a restaurant than a house.

"Thank you and your home is beautiful. This kitchen is amazing," she said looking around. She looked around and noticed all of the beautiful art, something she enjoyed looking at also.

"Thank you. It's definitely the kind of house I've always wanted."

Karen nodded remembering conversations in the past about houses and he described one that looked a lot like this one.

"I especially love all of the beautiful artwork you have, even here in the kitchen."

"Thank you," he said coming around the counter to greet her with a luscious kiss.

"I needed that," she said.

"I was on business recently in Boston and accompanied a client to an art gallery showing of a local artist named Zora Michaels. I purchased a few of her pieces, which are the ones you see here in the kitchen. I needed something bold in this room because it's one of my favorite rooms in the house. When people ask me why I needed such a big house when I live alone, I tell them I needed to have it big enough to fit around the kitchen I wanted."

"You always did love to cook Thomas. I never knew when you had the time."

"Well, I have plenty of time now. I don't cook as often as I'd like to, but it's not because I don't have the time anymore. One reason is because I have the best cook in the world and I love her cooking, but I do love being in the kitchen cooking up new dishes. What about you? Do you still love to bake?" he asked.

Karen sat down at the island in the middle of the room, across from where he was slicing vegetables.

"I do, though I haven't had time to do much baking."

"Well, maybe you can bake something for me soon."

She liked the sound of that. To her, he was planning on them spending a lot of time together and was opening up his life and kitchen to her. That said something.

"I'd like that. Can I help you do anything?" she asked.

Thomas didn't reply, but gave her a sly, hooded look with his eyes. She read that look immediately and chuckled at his voracious sexual appetite, something she could never tire of.

"I'm talking about something besides that and more about dinner. We'll have time for that later," she said with a sexy undertone.

"You promise?" he said almost begging.

"I promise. Now, as for dinner, what can I do?" she asked.

"You can finish the salad while I check on the lamb chops and asparagus, your favorite vegetable."

They talked while they cooked.

"I'm glad you invited me over," she said.

"I'm happy you accepted. I want to tell you that I haven't been this happy in a long time. I'm glad you're back in Raleigh."

She looked at him and the sincerity in his words, hit her like a brick. To her they were the Karen and Thomas of old and because of how in love they had been, it was easy to fall back into their current routine of spending quality time together. The difference is, this time, they weren't worried about chasing careers; they were focused on each other. Though the case crept up in her mind, she decided to put it to the side for the night and focus on the time they had. She hoped it would continue after the case, but there was no way to tell until after the case was over and she revealed everything to him.

"I'm glad you were still here. I've thought about you over the years, wondering how life had turned out for you and if you were happy."

"Well, for years, I think I was content because I was focused on building my brand and my business. I can say that I am extremely happy now and a lot of that is due to you. I've missed the kind of connection you and I share. It's open, honest, loving and of course hotter than ever. I would be crazy to not be happy. What about you?" he asked.

Hearing him tell her what's in his heart made her feel even more like a woman on a case than a woman in love and she hated that. She still wanted to be honest about her feelings, which were true, case or not.

"I'm happy and that happiness is because of you. I never thought we'd be here ever again and I'm happy to know that I could be wrong about that."

"Well, I'm glad I have something to do with that. Now, dinner is pretty much done if you want to start moving everything into the dining room, which is on the other side of this wall. I'll get everything else from the oven," he said.

Karen shivered at how domestic they were, knowing this is what she'd always wanted for them. Still, in the back of her mind, the case stood out like a sore thumb.

"I can do that," she said.

**

Carl yawned after sitting in his car a few car-lengths down from Thomas large estate. He wasn't planning to spend hours sitting there waiting, but when he saw Karen pass by as he finished pumping gas in his car, his sixth-sense told him to follow her. He didn't trust her after he discovered she and Thomas were secretly seeing each other. He had also become suspicious of the friendship Karen had developed with Liza and she seemed to be asking a lot of questions. Liza, he thought, was so stupid that she didn't catch on that he was digging into their friendship by asking her questions that revealed lot of what she and Karen had been talking about. To him, Karen was asking more about him than just having girl-talk. He also had other suspicions about her when he discovered she was more intelligent than she wanted anyone to believe. She was working at Atwater Industries for other reasons besides the one she wanted them all to believe and he had a feeling it was more than the fact that she was screwing the boss. Something else was going on and the uncomfortable feeling he had about her led him to follow her, which led him to Thomas' house.

After hours of sitting outside in the dark waiting, it was obvious Karen wasn't going to come out any time soon. There was more to Karen than what she let everyone in on and he intended to find out. What if she came across something about what he'd been doing? What if Liza had let something slip? If that were the case, then he would have to change his timeline of leaving the country, but not before taking care of Karen. He couldn't leave any loose ends behind. He had worked too hard to hide any trace of the money he'd been stealing and if Karen knew anything, he needed to find out and perhaps he could still get away before anyone else found out.

Carl put his car in drive and was about to pull off when his cell phone rang and he snatched it up seeing Liza's number.

"What do you want Liza?" he grunted out.

"Wow, what's wrong, baby?"

"Nothing is wrong. You caught me at a busy time."

Carl softened his tone so that he didn't throw her off and he didn't want to sit in this affluent neighborhood. Anyone could walk by and he didn't want to be caught sitting there.

"Well, I was calling to see if I was going to see you tonight. You told me to stay home tonight because you were coming over. I've been sitting here waiting, naked and ready for you, Carl. Are you coming?" Liza said, almost purring in the phone.

Hearing the spiciness of her voice, he could imagine what was waiting for him and he was so stressed out that he could use the release. Picturing Liza with her large breasts and satiny soft thighs open and waiting for him, he had to shift in the car seat to adjust the pressure behind his zipper. He looked towards Thomas' house again before deciding to go visit Liza. He would deal with Karen later. Hopefully, she was more innocent than he thought and he wouldn't have to hurt her. If he needed to, he would if it meant he could get out of Raleigh with his nest egg.

"I'm on my way. Keep it tight for me. I'll be there in a few minutes," he said, pulling into the road and heading towards her apartment.

13

Dinner had been remarkable and Thomas was glad he'd finally invited her out to his house. They had spent all of their time together either at her house or at the apartment he kept near to the office, especially on nights when he worked late and didn't feel like driving out to his home. It was closer and more convenient for them to be together. He invited her out to spend the night and since she didn't have to go in the office tomorrow and he could work from home, he decided to make it a romantic night at his house. Thomas wanted her to see all of who he was now and this house was a large part of him. It's where he spent most of his time when he wasn't at the office.

Following dinner, they agreed to relax and watch a movie. To him, life was as close to perfect as they could get. He was given a second chance with her and he wasn't going to blow it. One of the reasons they split many years ago, was because he didn't set enough time aside for them and they weren't his priority. He's hoping to prove that he's a different person now and if given the chance, he wants more than just sex and nights alone like this; he wanted forever.

Karen took in the entire evening of dinner and snuggling and the case was far from her mind. They cuddled, kissed, caressed and pretended to be focused on the movie though she knew he was probably thinking some of the same thoughts as she was; that they were in love again. She knew she was risking a lot, but she wanted him to know what was in her heart.

"Thomas?" she said against his chest where she was currently laying her head.

"Yes, baby," he said giving her a soft kiss on the forehead. He looked down as she looked up at him with every bit of love he longed to see.

"I love you," she proclaimed and waited for his reaction.

Thomas didn't hesitate even a second before responding.

"I love you, too, baby. It took us a long time to get here, but we are."

Karen sat up so that they could really talk.

"You are still the man I've dreamed about my whole life. I know we can't go back and change the past, but since I've been back here in Raleigh, I've often wished that I could and we wouldn't have wasted so many precious years. If I've never said it before, I need to say it now; I'm sorry for the years gone by. We could have been much more if all of that hadn't happened. I don't, however, want to continue looking back. I want to move forward and see what our life can be like now."

Karen was risking a lot because deep down, she knew she was living a lie as long as she continued to keep the full truth from him. The evening was magical and she felt like it wasn't the time to put everything out on the table. In case things didn't turn out well, she wanted this time with him.

"Karen, baby, I can't imagine going back to a life without you. I don't plan on wasting any more time in the past either. I want to live in the here and now with you. You mean everything to me and I plan to make sure you always know that and that you never doubt it. Never again will you fear not being first in my life. You are first and the only thing that matters to me right now. If I lost everything today and still had you, I would still be as happy as I am right this minute and I owe that all to you," he admitted.

Karen's heart melted and her voice felt about to crack.

"I love you so much," she said before not missing the chance to meld her mouth to his as he came closer, sealing their love in a powerful connection.

When they felt the kiss getting out of control, they turned off the movie and headed to the bedroom. It was time to not only seal their love with a kiss, but to join their bodies as one, allowing their love to flow between them.

As they joined each other and their love on the

bed, Thomas reached for Karen first. Tonight, he would take his time and make love to every part of her body. He started first with her lips before venturing down to capture her breasts in his mouth, loving the sound of her soft cries as her body reacted to his touch. He was at the height of his excitement knowing that he had Karen in his home and in his bed.

Thomas traced her body with his tongue from one end to the other, stopping to pay special attention to sensitive spots along the way. She moaned low when his hands caressed her, kneading her flesh, making it come alive as only he could. When he was ready, he slowly slid between her legs and without being able to wait any longer, he wrapped her legs around his waist and thrust deep, burying himself inside her tight sheath as far as he could go.

Karen held her breath, bracing herself for the influx of erotic pleasure she knew would flood her body, mind and soul and Thomas being inside of her didn't disappoint. As he moved inside of her, she moved her hips with him as he started with a slow pace that caused her to impatiently wiggle under him, trying to encourage him to put out the fire that had started low, between her legs and was now moving throughout her entire body. As he pushed inside of her while caressing the sensitive points of her breasts, Karen let out a moan as she threw her head from side to side, enjoying how

Thomas' plunges inside of her touched every pleasure point on her body.

"More, Thomas!" she begged.

"I know you want more baby, but let me love you. I don't want to rush this. I want to feel every stroke in and out of your body and I want to watch everything I make you feel show across your face."

To show what he meant, Thomas reached down and brought both of her legs up into the curve of his arms, raising and stretching them up alongside her head, giving him an even deeper penetration.

"Aww, yes!" Karen screamed.

Thomas increased his pace, grinding his hips making sure every pass into her body was felt in every fiber of her being. He then leaned down close to her ear, not missing a stroke inside of her.

"I told you I know what you want and need."

Karen delighted in the feel of Thomas strong body covering hers giving her body just what it wanted and needed. Her groans of pleasure caused her to uncontrollably rock her head from left to right even faster, dazed by the amount of pleasure she was receiving from him. Her body belonged to him, to do as he pleased and right now he appeared to want to focus on satisfying her thirst for him.

"I love how you make me feel. Don't ever stop Thomas," Karen whispered as he finally increased the pace to the point that the headboard of the bed began banging against the wall. To her, that sound was as erotic as the wet, slippery sounds their bodies were making as he pounded into her hard like she liked.

"Oh, Karen!" Thomas screamed when his passion for her overflowed.

"Yes baby, that's exactly what I need."

Karen shouted as Thomas went deeper, faster and much fiercer with his intent to drive her crazy.

Thomas continued making love to her, giving her deep, penetrating strokes which she met over and over again. The sounds of their love making were all they heard in the room and it was both stimulating and intoxicating. She was so aroused that Thomas' excitement grew as he easily slid in and out of her body, increasing the pace even more until they shattered together with spasms that rocked them to their core. The moaning Thomas heard, he thought was coming from Karen until he realized it was coming from him and he couldn't control it if he wanted to. He let loose as they became one.

They stayed resting like this with him on top, still connected to her intimately. Thomas knew he could stay like this all night. Pulling Karen as close to him as he could, he placed soft, light kisses all over her face as she stretched releasing a contented sigh. He knew how she felt as the feeling of pure satisfaction overtook him as well.

After a few minutes, Thomas noticed Karen's breathing had slowed and had become shallow. She had fallen asleep, with him still deep-seated inside of her body. He extricated himself and pulled her body in close to his as he also joined her in a deep and very satisfying slumber.

14

Happy was Karen's current mood, knowing that the case was almost over. She had all the proof she needed to convict Carl of embezzlement from Thomas' company. She just needed to make copies of the last few pages of the secret ledger that Carl was hiding. Besides the ledger, Karen had also discovered information that proved that he and Liza were planning to skip town very soon and so she needed to act quickly. She couldn't wait until they were in handcuffs and behind bars, so that she could finally come clean with Thomas about what the true reason was behind her being at his company. She hated deceiving him and there had been many occasions when she wanted to tell him, but didn't. Though she hated being dishonest, she couldn't risk blowing the case without knowing how he would react. He may approach Carl and could blow everything which could then not clear him of everything like she wanted.

Karen hated lying to him after they now have found their way back to each other again and if things were going to work for them this time, there couldn't be any secrets and this one was major. Once she finished making duplicates of each page of the ledger, she would pass the information on to the local agents who would then arrest Carl and Liza before they had a chance to leave town where it's possible they would never be seen or heard from again. Being in the office alone, she had to work quickly before anyone else came in.

Karen had stayed late for a reason only known to her and she'd given excuses to her team who offered to stay and help her work out some financial balances that she couldn't quite get done during the workday. After everyone had gone and Carl had stopped by unexpectedly asking strange questions, she was finally alone and finally had a chance to head to Carl's office. Now that she had the code to the safe in his office thanks to the recorder she'd placed in his office, she finally had her hand on what she needed. She made quick work of copying so that she could get out of the office before someone else, who may be working late in another part of the building, caught her and blew everything. She worked feverishly while checking to see that no one else was around.

**

Carl slipped back into the building through a rear entrance that he'd propped open in hopes of returning unnoticed to get what he needed out of his safe to finally disappear. Like a snake slithers, he moved from one hall to the next until he had his office in sight. He could hear the copy machine running and knew that someone else was still in the building and he had an inkling it was Karen. He would deal with her after he got what he needed.

The moment he walked into his office, he knew something was array. He looked toward the safe and noticed it was slightly ajar. He knew that it couldn't have been Liza because he'd walked her out with instructions to start packing because they were leaving in a few days. Walking over to the safe, he opened it and when he searched for the secret ledger, it was missing. That feeling he got that told him to go back to the building had paid off.

His day had started with following Karen around and questioning her about her movements around the office. A few times, he'd caught her snooping where she should not have been and though he didn't say anything at the time, he decided to continue watching her. What really had him thinking was that earlier in the day, while he was out of the office for most of the day, he had come back, opened his safe and things seemed to have been moved around. He did ask Liza about that and she told him it wasn't her. He wasn't sure who else it could have been, but that feeling that Karen wasn't who she said she was made him think about her and the chance that she could have been snooping and came upon his scheme. Due to his severe case of obsessive-compulsive disorder, he liked everything in its proper place and he knew that if Liza said she hadn't touched it, someone else had. He had to tell Liza of his suspicions when she told him that he had been acting strange. She was also surprised that he had moved the date up for them to leave the country. The only information he gave her was that he had a feeling Karen knew about the scheme and had used the ploy of befriending her in order to get more information. He didn't know if she was working with anyone or had alerted anyone to what was happening, but he would handle it and get back to her. Liza told him she was scared, but he assured her, they would be long gone before anything or anyone came down on them.

Carl knew he had to catch Karen off-guard and rather than wait for her to return to put the ledger back in his safe, he instead headed to her office where he knew she would need to return to grab her things before leaving. He slipped out of his office quietly and walked toward her office to wait. He would let her explain and then dispose of her in her own office so that it wouldn't be linked to him. There would be enough suspicion once the missing money was discovered after he and Liza were gone.

**

Thomas had just about reached his house when he realized he had gotten so caught up in phone sex with Karen after he'd left the office while she was locked in hers, that he'd left the papers for his morning meeting that he wanted to look over. His plan was to return to the office, but the erotic encounter over the phone had exhausted him and he turned in the direction of his house. He thought for a minute that he could swing by in the morning to grab them, but the office was in the opposite direction from where he was meeting a client in the morning. It wouldn't take him long to go back to the office quickly and since it was late and the roads would be clear, he could be back home in no time. He turned around and headed back to the office, saving himself time in the morning.

**

Liza paced around her living room nervous as she thought about what could be happening to Karen. After talking to Carl, she thought back over the conversations she and Karen had and realized Karen had been pumping her for information in a sly way. According to Carl, Karen had been faking an interest in a real friendship while trying to get information on Carl. Even if that were true, she believed there was a true friendship with Karen and had a hard time believing it was all a lie. She was afraid of what Carl had planned to do to Karen and had a feeling it wasn't going to turn out well.

Her love for Carl was real, though she knew he saw her as more of arm candy than a real love interest. She knew he loved all of the kinky things she allowed him to do to her, which were all of the things his wife wouldn't do. It may be a sick kind of love because sometimes Carl could be a real pig, but he filled a void she needed. She normally wouldn't go for a man like him who flirted with every skirt he saw and the fact that he was married should have also been a deterrent, but she was about to have more money than she'd ever had in her life and for that, she could deal with Carl at least until the money ran out.

Liza knew that she had spent years being poor and not having any money because she lived way beyond her means. She needed Carl and she had done some unspeakable and rather creepy sex things just to keep him interested in her. She may have been using her body to get what she needed and wanted, but men were stupid, too. Throw a little tail their way and they would do just about anything to keep getting more of it. Murder though, is not something she signed up for.

It wouldn't bother her so much if she didn't like Karen. She was the only person at the company who saw past Liza's exterior and told her she could be much more than a doormat for any man, especially one who is married and have no problem cheating on his wife. Liza had begun to enjoy the friendship with Karen even after Carl told her to stay away from her because he thought she was becoming suspicious of their behavior. Liza couldn't let Carl hurt her. She wasn't sure all the money in the world would help her forget that she would be an accomplice to murder. She had to stop him or at least talk him out of it. She searched her purse for her cell phone and called him several times, each time the call went straight to his voicemail which means that he most likely had turned his phone off. She had to convince him to let it go, get the money and leave. They had stolen enough money from the company that they could live brand new lives where no one would find them and there was no need to bring even more heat down on them by hurting Karen. Instead of packing like he told her too, she grabbed her keys to head back to the office, which was only a few blocks away. Adrenaline pumped through her as she hurried and prayed she would get there in time before Carl hurt Karen. She knew that Karen was staying late at the office and Carl was headed back up to the office to get the books. That would leave them there alone. She moved faster in hopes of getting there before Carl did something that they wouldn't be able to run far enough from.

Liza locked her door and rather than wait for the elevator in her building, she ran down the stairs in a sweat suit and tennis, jumped in her car and sped out of the parking lot.

15

Karen had finally finished making the copies that she needed and was headed back to her office to grab her things before placing the ledger back in Carl's safe before leaving and heading straight for the FBI building. The original plan was for her to get proof, fax it over and then the FBI would swoop in without compromising who she was and arrest Carl and Liza. She changed that plan because she wanted to be able to talk to Thomas before all hell broke loose in his office tomorrow morning. After dropping the proof off, her plan was to call Thomas from the car and ask to see him where she would lay everything out for him and beg for his forgiveness for deceiving him. She had to try and in the morning, when things came down, they could begin to rebuild their trust again in hopes that she could get him to understand why she had to keep things from him.

She quickly entered her office, grabbed her purse and keys while holding onto the ledger and her copies which she'd placed in a folder. She had already reached out to one of the FBI agents to let them know she would be at the office under an hour with everything they would need to arrest Carl. Taking one last look at her desk to make sure she had everything, she turned around to leave when the door to her office almost closed, revealing Carl standing behind it. Karen couldn't move as all kinds of thoughts went through her mind, starting with the fact that she had the ledger in her hand and Carl's eyes went straight to it before they locked eyes.

"What are you doing, Karen?" he said with venom spewing with every word he spoke. Carl looked again at the ledger in her hand.

"Why are you in my office hiding behind the door?" Karen stumbled out while she thought of her next move which involved getting by him.

"Is that what you're worried about? Is that my ledger I see in your hands you sneaky little liar? I knew you were up to something."

Carl started moving closer to Karen as she backed up closer to her desk contemplating how to get out of her current situation.

"Nothing to say?" he snarled.

Karen realized she needed to keep him focused on talking while she figured out what to do. There was also no need to lie anymore since he'd pretty much caught her red-handed with the ledger in her hand. She could lie and say it was Thomas', but she had a feeling he already knew it was the one from his safe.

"It's over Carl and I know what you've been doing," she said.

"Oh, you do, do you? So, you're gonna run and tell your boyfriend Thomas? Was that your next move? I don't think so because you'll be dead before you get across the room to this door," he said matter-of-factly.

Karen could feel the vile-filled anger in every word he spoke. She became increasingly scared as she watched him produce a gun from behind his back. His presence and actions were unexpected and this was beyond a seriously dangerous situation. She knew he was a thief, but she didn't peg him as a killer.

"Carl, don't be stupid. Put the gun down," she said trying to sound convincing.

"Or what? I take it no one even knows you're here. Don't worry your pretty little head because you won't feel a thing. I'm a pretty good shot and I'll make it quick and lethal on the first shot," he said as he pointed the gun right at her head.

Karen needed to keep him talking long enough for her to reach down and push the button on her hip. She had been given the small device by the FBI in case she was in a dangerous situation and needed help right away. One push and the FBI would be alerted to her location and would come to her aid. Right now, she had her hands up in surrender and they were filled with the items she'd picked up from her desk. If she kept him talking, she may be able to reason with him long enough to drop her hands and press her signal.

"Don't you want to know why I'm here Carl? What I found?" she said hoping to distract him.

"Yeah, I do."

"I know you've been stealing money from the company and I know that Liza has been helping you hide it from everyone. Why Carl? Why would you steal from Thomas after how good he's been to you over the years?" she said, pleading for an answer.

"Oh what, so now you're looking out for your boyfriend right? His company makes plenty of money, so he won't miss the little bit I'm taking. Insurance will cover the money from the retirement funds."

"Carl, that money belongs to the employees. The amount of money you are stealing, you won't be able to run far enough away that they're not going to look for you. You need to turn yourself in. You don't really want to hurt me. You're just overwhelmed by the circumstances of what you've done. I'm sure the FBI will go easier on you if you turn yourself in."

Karen realized her mistake the moment the words left her mouth.

FBI? Carl wondered what the FBI had to do with anything. Had she alerted them to what he was doing? Who was she? He thought.

This was bad. Carl started pacing while keeping

the gun pointed at Karen's head. He was in a lot of trouble if she had already told the authorities.

"FBI? You contacted the FBI? What the hell did you tell them Karen? I need to know what you said to them," he said angrily.

Karen didn't mean to agitate him more. She needed to get to the button on her hip. She started talking to him while moving slowly to put the items down on her desk.

"Here, Carl. Here is your ledger. Take it and get out of here while you can," she said placing it on the desk, freeing up one of her hands. Carl looked down at it.

The little bit of distracting worked because it only took her a split second to push the button at her waist to send a signal. Now she just had to continue to distract him until assistance arrived.

"I have to kill you Karen or I'll never get away now," he said, leveling the gun at her.

**

Liza walked up to Karen's office where she could hear Carl and Karen arguing. Karen was pleading with Carl to give himself up and clearly Carl was out of his mind not knowing what to do. Liza knew she had to stop him before he went down a path they could never recover from. Without thinking, she pushed the door to Karen's office open a little more as Carl started explaining that he couldn't let her go because she knew too much and he needed time to get away. If he let her go, she would go straight to the police and he couldn't have that.

Karen and Carl both looked at Liza as she entered the room. Karen knew she could have an opportunity to overpower Carl, but now that Liza was in the room, she couldn't risk getting her shot.

"Liza, what are you doing here? I told you to pack and be ready to leave after I take care of our nosey bookkeeper here. I sent you a text that we were leaving tonight instead of in a few days. You shouldn't be here. Go do what I said, NOW!" he shouted, clearly agitated.

Nervously, Liza moved closer to him.

"Carl, I'm not leaving. Let Karen go," she pleaded.

Carl looked at Karen.

"I can't do that."

"Carl, we can take the money we have and get out of town right now. Let's just go. This is going too far," she said with fear in her eyes.

"I'm sorry Liza, but I can't do that. She knows everything. She stole the ledger from my safe and I bet she even knows where we're headed because she has been snooping around for weeks. I kept all of that in the safe and as you can see from her desk, she has the ledger, so she saw everything else too. I'm sorry, but I can't let her go. Don't you see we have to kill her? By the time anyone finds her, we'll be long gone," he said, turning back to Karen, looking like he was about to pull the trigger.

Carl was sweating profusely and with the wild,

out of control look in his eyes, Karen was now frightened. She hoped the signal worked and her team were on their way.

**

Thomas pulled up to the office and noticed not only Karen's car in the parking lot, but Carl's and Liza's as well. He knew he was the last to leave for the evening other than Karen who was leaving shortly after he did, so he didn't know why the three of them would have returned. He got out of his car and made his way into the building.

As he reached Karen's office to see why she was still there, he noticed not only the light on, but he heard several voices. One voice he heard was Carl's talking extremely loud and angry and he could also hear Liza and Karen pleading with him. He was about to go into the office when he heard Carl say something about killing Karen because she was a sneak and a liar. He wondered what was going on and before he barged in, he needed to know what the situation was. Adrenaline was pumping strong through his body as he struggled with going inside or waiting for the right moment to barge in. He didn't know what was on the other side of the door waiting for him.

Karen figured she only needed to distract Carl a little longer and this would all be over. Maybe it was time to enter a little fear into the equation.

"Carl, listen to me, okay? You won't be able to get away with this."

CHERYL BARTON

"Like hell I won't. Liza here won't say anything and if you had said anything to anyone by now, you wouldn't have had to sneak back in here tonight to make copies of my information, so yeah, I do believe I'm about to get away with this," he boasted.

It was time she came clean, Karen thought. It was probably the only way to save her own life. Surely Carl wouldn't kill an FBI agent.

"No, Carl, you're not. I'm not who you think I am. Don't make this worse than it is right now."

Carl's face turned ashen, almost white.

"What do you mean you're not who I think you are? Who I think you are is a nosey, rotten little snoop of a bookkeeper who has been screwing her boss to get ahead," he spit out.

"No, Carl, I'm not. In fact, I'm not a bookkeeper at all. I'm actually an FBI agent."

That bit of news not only shocked Carl and Liza, but Thomas as well who was listening on the other side of the door.

He stood glued to the spot, not being able to move after Karen's admission. He peeped in the crack in the door and wondered how he could get in and diffuse the situation.

"You're what?" Carl questioned, now showing more fear and a little less anger.

"You heard me, Carl. I'm an FBI agent and I've been working here undercover because the FBI suspected Thomas of embezzling money from his own company. I was sent in to uncover evidence for

166

a conviction, so you see if you kill me, you're not killing a bookkeeper that you think no one will care about. You would be charged with murdering a federal officer and for that, you could get the death penalty and you don't want that. Please put the gun down, let me call for some help and you only have to deal with the embezzlement charge," she pleaded.

"Listen to her Carl. This has gone too far," Liza added.

"Shut up Liza. I need to think," he said.

Thomas couldn't believe his ears. Karen was an FBI agent, working undercover in his company to find evidence to convict him of embezzlement? He couldn't think clearly. He didn't understand what was going on. He didn't have time to react to the news, but instead he knew he needed to get in there and keep Carl from killing her. He would deal with the information he revealed about herself later.

Just before he was about to enter her office, he saw movement to his right. When he turned, he saw men in riot gear with guns pointed at him. One of the men approaching signaled for him to be quiet and to move away from the door. They were listening just as he was to the conversation happening on the other side of the door.

Thomas moved away as, what he assumed were federal agents, moved closer to the door. One of the men peeped inside to assess the situation and when he realized they could proceed, he signaled with his hands and he rushed the room, placing himself in front of Karen, announcing himself as an FBI agent, shouting for Carl to drop his weapon.

Carl saw not only that agent, but others were entering the room as well. He saw no way out, so defeated, he slowly lowered his gun and himself to the floor. One of the agents rushed to subdue him while the other kicked the gun out of Carl's reach.

Karen could breathe easier now knowing that this was over. She was about to thank the agents when she saw Thomas standing in the doorway. He had a look on his face that told her he'd heard her admission about being an agent undercover. She thought she saw fear, but that was immediately replaced with hurt. He was taking in everything and he knew she had been lying to him all along. Holding off her concern for Thomas, she did what she had been trained to do which was to pull out her FBI badge and place it around her neck so that she could easily be identified as an agent.

The hurt in Thomas' eyes told the story of what she would have to deal with in her explanation to him and deep down, she had a feeling no explanation would repair what was probably now over between them. This isn't how she wanted him to find out about her. Her original plan was that this was going to be the night when she was going to tell him everything, not have him find out this way. She was about to say something to him when one of the agents came up to her as she kept her eyes on Thomas and his were still on her. Thomas still hadn't moved or said a word.

"Great job, Agent Jacobs. Your director is on his way in and asked that I tell you to hang around for him. He just touched down on his flight from Washington and should be here any minute."

Karen wanted to deal with a stunned Thomas, but she still had a job to do.

"Here are the files and ledger you'll need to charge Carl. Liza here is also an accomplice, though I'd like to be sure and add to my report that she showed up tonight to help me."

One of the agents took the items from her while the other told Thomas he needed to speak with him privately and escorted Thomas down the hall to one of the other offices.

Karen's last thought as Thomas walked away was though the case turned out well, this just blew up in her face.

16

The chair Karen was sitting in outside of the office where several FBI agents, including her director were talking to Thomas, started to feel like brick. It wasn't, but she was nervous and tired of sitting and waiting. They were inside letting him know that he was in the clear and that in the morning they would be holding a press conference for the media and they needed him present so that they could make it clear that though he had been the main suspect, he was now in the clear thanks to the diligent work of Agent Karen Jacobs. She was imagining Thomas cringing at the mentioning of her name. Karen could have left, but she didn't. She had to make Thomas hear her out and she couldn't leave before talking to him to clear everything up.

She stood up and began pacing and thinking through what her next move would be. She loved Thomas and she didn't want to go back to a life without him.

Sitting back down, she sat straight up when the door to the office opened and everyone poured out.

She stood and her eyes went straight to Thomas whose eyes locked onto hers. Karen was afraid when she didn't see love or compassion. She saw a man who had been hurt by her lies and deceit and she didn't know how to handle that. It was clear that her betrayal was devastating to him. She knew that she was the last person he wanted to see or hear from, but she had to try. She couldn't let him leave and have the night to stew over all that she had done and all that they had done since she arrived back in Raleigh, knowing it was all built on a lie.

"Karen," her boss said addressing her.

"Yes, sir?" she replied, keeping her eyes on Thomas.

"I'm going to let you get some rest tonight, but I want you in the field office early in the morning for a briefing ahead of the press conference that we'll do from the office. Congratulations on a job well done," he said before heading towards the door.

As everyone walked away, Karen was left standing in the aisle with Thomas who had not moved or said anything to her. She wasn't sure how to proceed, but she had to say something.

"Thomas, let me explain."

It was clear he didn't want to hear anything she had to say when while she spoke, he turned and headed for the exit. For a few steps, she let him go and didn't follow. She knew if he left with the thoughts that were on his mind about what she'd done, he would never forgive her. She needed to make him understand she did this for him. She loved him and she would never do anything to hurt him. She followed behind him to the parking lot.

Thomas was angry, hurt and disgusted. He could hear Karen's footsteps behind him, but he wasn't turning around. He needed to get as far away from her as he possibly could. The last thing he wanted to do was talk to her after the lie she'd been living for two months.

"Please, let me explain," Karen said coming up behind him while continuing to plead with him. As soon as Thomas reached his car, she came close enough and reached out to touch his arm. It shocked her when he pulled away from her as if she were someone he despised. That action wounded her to the core.

"Don't touch me," he said with so much revolt in his voice, it stunned her into silence.

"I'm sorry," she said softly.

"Stop talking to me and don't touch me again. You have nothing to say that I want to hear, Agent Karen Jacobs," he spat out like it was poison in his mouth.

She had to get her say in while she had the chance.

"I love you, Thomas. That was real; my love is real. I didn't mean to hurt you and I'm sorry," she said with as much emotion as she could muster.

The nerve of her, Thomas thought to himself as

he finally turned around to face her. He needed to face her and get this over with because he never wanted to have to deal with her again.

"Sorry? You're sorry? Wait, so let me see if I can figure out what you're sorry about. You're sorry that you betrayed me. You're sorry that you lied to me. You're sorry that you have lived a complete lie with me for the past few months. Is that it? Maybe you're sorry that you had to sleep with me to get close enough to me to try and find information to bring me up on charges?" Thomas could see that got a rise out of her.

"That's not true," she said on the verge of tears.

"Wait, let me finish. You wanted to talk, so we're talking. Maybe you're sorry that you've harbored such vengeful thoughts for me all these years that you couldn't pass up the chance to pose as a bookkeeper to try and set me up for a fall? Was that it? You've hated me so much all these years that you would do this to me? You declared your love for me. You made love to me like nothing and no one existed in the world, but you and me. Was that a lie, too? I feel sick that I let you get close to me again. I should have known it wasn't a coincidence that you just happened to be in my favorite restaurant sitting at a table right across from me where I wouldn't be able to miss you. Yes, your boss told me it was all a set-up. I was so caught up in seeing you again that I didn't think anything of it. I'm thinking back over everything that the agents told me and everything that has gone on between us for the past few months and I feel like I need to take a shower. No, you don't get to explain because I already know enough to last me a lifetime. You disgust me and you are a pathetic liar. I never want to see or talk to you again, Agent Jacobs and as much as I wanted to, I didn't tell them about all the times you screamed my name in the past two months. I doubt that would go over well with your superiors or was it their idea for you to go that far?" he asked.

Karen didn't know what to say. Thomas had never spoken to her that way before and she was at a loss for words.

Thomas didn't wait around to hear any more. He opened his car door, got in and sped off before she could get another word out.

Left standing in the same spot long after he had pulled away, Karen was crushed watching the man she loved drive out of her life. She didn't know what to do or where to go. She was lost. His last words burned a hole in her heart that she knew would never, ever heal. The man she loved more than life itself just told her he never wanted to see or talk to her again and she knew he meant every word. She turned toward her own car, fighting back the tears that were threatening to fall. The tears were filling up in her eyes and when they fell to her cheek, she let loose and cried. She sat crying for what seemed hours before putting her car in drive and going home to an empty house.

Karen drove through the streets of Raleigh, crying for everything that she'd just lost. It didn't take her long and when she pulled up, she saw her neighbor. She would normally park in the driveway, get out and converse with him, but not tonight. Tonight, she deserved to be alone after what she did.

She pulled into the garage and quickly exited the car to go inside. Passing by a mirror as she entered her house, she noticed that her eyes were bloodshot red. She had been crying nonstop all the way home, wondering how things had gotten so bad. She thought Thomas would be relieved to know that she did everything because she believed in his innocence. That didn't matter because he wouldn't allow her to explain her side. She didn't know how to fix the situation. She needed to talk to someone. She needed to talk to Lacey. She went in search of her laptop to see if Lacey was on-line. She logged in and opened up the video chat application they used.

She didn't see Lacey logged in as was the ritual they had lately for Karen to let her know how the case was going and how things were going with Thomas. She sent her a quick text to tell her to log in and after waiting a few minutes, Lacey appeared on the screen. Karen tried to smile, but the moment she saw Lacey's smile, she broke out in uncontrollable, body-wracking cries.

"Kay, sweetie, what's wrong? I need you to stop crying and tell me what's going on?" Lacey said with fear in her voice, while trying to remain calm.

Karen couldn't help herself as she cried out loud.

"Karen," Lacey said with a little more force. "Talk to me, you're scaring me."

Karen tried to gather herself enough to respond and finally found her voice.

"He hates me Lace. He told me I disgust him and he hates me," she said and then began to cry again.

"Whoa, who hates you and said you disgust them? Thomas?" Lacey asked.

Karen shook her head yes, not being able to speak.

"Okay, tell me what's going on. Where is he? Is he there with you? What happened?"

Karen took a few moments to get herself together enough to explain and proceeded to tell Lacey all that transpired over the past few hours, especially her conversation with Thomas in the parking garage.

"I can't shake the look on his face when he looked at me. I'll never be able to forget that look."

"I know you love him and you have to find a way to make him listen to you. After the press conference tomorrow, why don't you try to talk to him again. Perhaps he would have calmed down by then after a night of thinking things through. He has to see that you did this for him and not against him."

"I thought the same thing, but I don't believe he sees things that way. I betrayed him by keeping all of this from him and he'll never forgive me," Karen said, somberly.

"I'm coming to Raleigh tomorrow as soon as I can get a flight out. You need me," Lacey said.

"No, Lacey. You have your own life to deal with and I dug this ditch that I'm in. Besides, I don't think I'm going to stick around for the press conference. I need to get away from here as soon as possible. I'm hoping to get a flight out in the morning."

"Oh sweetie, I'm so sorry it turned out like this. I think if you waited a few days to let him cool off, you'll be able to explain how you did all of this because you knew he wasn't guilty and you needed to prove that to your higher ups who clearly thought that he was guilty. Give it a few days Karen and if you don't have to go back to Washington, D.C., right away, stay and work this out. You two have been so happy lately that I can't believe given time and a lot of explaining, you can't get through this. You can if you don't run away. It's time to stop running Karen. Stay and deal with this."

Karen couldn't do it. Running through her mind over and over again were the last words Thomas spoke to her. She needed to go home and get away from Raleigh.

"Thanks Lace, but I'm going home. Listen I'm feeling a little better now. I'm going to try and get some sleep because I have to do a briefing very early and then I'm getting on the road if I can't get a flight out. I'll call you when I get home. I love you and thanks for always listening."

Lacey knew she wasn't going to be able to change her mind, so she opted for being supportive.

"I love you too and if you need to talk to me anymore tonight, you call me. I don't care what time it is. I'm here for you. I will expect a call in the morning, okay?"

Karen nodded.

After the call was over, she knew she wouldn't be sleeping. Rather than look for a flight, she decided she would drive back home, needing the time to think about the last few months. As she headed to her room to pack, the look on Thomas' face continued to haunt her. She was tired of hurting him over and over. She would do what he asked and not be any place where he would have to see or talk to her again.

17

The press conference was about to begin and Thomas was ready. He hadn't slept a wink the night before, unable to digest what a fool he was for trusting Karen again with his heart. He looked around and didn't see her anywhere, which was fine with him because he had enough to deal with in the light of day and focusing on her wasn't in his plans.

The federal agent in charge went to the microphone in front of the press that had been called to the location. Thomas listened as the agent gave background on the case and how after careful execution of a great plan by one of their top agents, the true culprit was found and will be prosecuted. When he was done, Thomas listened as the man he remembered as Karen's boss stood at the podium to speak next. What he said shocked Thomas. Her director, Agent Jackson, commended Karen for a job well done. He also explained how from the first day, Karen knew that the owner, he, Thomas, was not guilty. Even when everyone else assumed the worst about him, she set out to prove them all wrong because she knew enough about him to know that he would and could never steal from his own employees.

To say he was shocked to hear that would be far from his original assessment of the situation. Even as agents gave him the rundown on everything the night before, none had mentioned that form the start, Karen knew he was innocent and that she set out to prove it because she knew the kind of man he was. Paying attention, he learned from the press conference that even though with her connection to the town and to Thomas, she could have turned down the assignment, but she didn't believe that anyone else would seek out another person, but that they would probably look to pin it on the owner whom she knew without a doubt was innocent. Agent Jackson ended by saying he was glad he was wrong in his initial assessment that Thomas was guilty. He was also proud to announce that all of the money stolen had been recovered and would be returned to the employees' retirement fund.

When it was Thomas' time to speak, he thanked the FBI for their hard work because if it had not been for them, it was possible Carl would have gotten away and he could have possibly been in jail himself.

The agents took a few questions from the media before the press conference was disbursed. Thomas thanked them again and headed to his office to calm employees he knew would be wondering what was going on. In the back of his mind, he realized, Karen hadn't really betrayed him. She had lied to him, but for good cause. She was trying to prove he was innocent and she started on the path to proving him innocent before they had slept together and before they had fallen in love again. He felt horrible for the things he'd said to her the night before. In the light of day and after the press conference, everything was clear. The bad thing about it was that he couldn't take back any of the things he'd said to her. He was sorry and possibly, with the right amount of begging, she would listen to him. He could only hope.

After dealing with a staff that was now calm and ready to get back to work, Thomas went into his own office and tried several times to reach out to Karen even though he had yet to dial all of the digits of her phone. He hung up each time before he got to the last number. He didn't know what to say that would erase the hateful words he'd said the night before. He still loved her, but he knew she may not believe that after the things he'd said. First, he would get a memo out to everyone on what their next steps at the company would be and then he would get back to figuring his life out with Karen.

**

Lacey walked into Thomas' office building trying to calm her attitude down before confronting him about his treatment of her best friend. She didn't want to see Karen make that same mistake again and she also knew how much Thomas loved Karen. If it were possible, she believed he actually loved her more now than he did before. Letting them both continue to make the biggest mistake of their lives was not an option which was why she waited a few days and then flew to Raleigh to talk to him. No way was Karen going to reach out to him again to repair things, so she was going to Thomas in hopes that he would take the first step.

She was glad to hear that Carl had been indicted for embezzling money from the retirement accounts and she remembered watching the press conference and saw that Karen was noticeably absent from the scene where she should have been to get the credit for the work she did. Now that the business side of things was squared away, it was time for the personal side to be built back up.

Lacey walked up to the receptionist in the lobby of Thomas' building to see if he was in the office.

"Good morning. Is there something I can help you with?" the receptionist asked.

"Yes, my name is Lacey Dawson and I'd like to see Mr. Atwater if he's available please."

"Is Mr. Atwater expecting you?"

"No, I'm a friend of his in town for today only and I was hoping I could catch him while I was here."

"Let me check with his assistant to see if he's in."

"Thank you," Lacey replied.

She listened as the receptionist confirmed

whether Thomas was in and if he had time to see her. It gave her a little more time to get her emotions in check so that she didn't come off too angry or aggressive when talking to him. She wanted her words to be compassionate and not demanding or accusatory.

"Mr. Atwater is in and said to send you up. You can take the elevators on your left to the fourth floor and his assistant Ms. Ellis will take you in."

"Thank you very much," Lacey said and headed towards the elevator.

"Ms. Dawson?" the assistant greeted Lacey as she stepped off when the elevator reached the floor.

"Yes," Lacey said extending her hand to return the greeting.

"Mr. Atwater is waiting for you in his office, so if you'll follow me, please?"

Lacey followed her on shaky legs. She knew that she needed to handle this correctly. Her friend's happiness depended on it.

Thomas looked up as his assistant entered his office followed by Lacey.

"Mr. Atwater, Ms. Dawson to see you."

"Thank you, Connie."

As his assistant left he stood as Lacey came closer.

"Connie, could you close the door behind you and hold my calls and visits for now, please?" He then turned his attention to Lacey.

"Lacey, it's good to see you again."

"Hi, Thomas. I'm sorry to intrude, but I was hoping we could talk if you had the time."

"Sure, have a seat," he gestured.

Lacey took a seat on the leather seat in front of his desk as he retook his seat behind it.

"What can I do for you Lacey?" he inquired, having a feeling he knew why she was here, but decided to let her tell him instead.

"Karen," was all she said.

"What about her?" he asked.

"Thomas, we've known each other a lot of years, yes?"

"Yes."

"You also know that if no one else in the world knows your history with Karen, it's me."

"Yes, I know that too," he replied.

"We've been out of touch for a lot of years, but I still consider you a friend."

"Lacey, I feel the same way," he admitted.

"Good, because as your friend, I just want to say, I think you're being a jackass."

Lacey could see the shock that registered on Thomas' face when he realized she'd just called him a jackass.

Before he could respond, Lacey put her hand up to stop him.

"Let me finish before you interrupt me, okay?"

Thomas shook his head and let her continue.

Lacey braced herself for the speech that she hoped would light a fire under him and get him to make the move that would lead to him and Karen having their fairytale ending.

"I watched my friend walk away from you before and I know firsthand it was the hardest thing she's ever had to do. Well, that is before this new fiasco with the FBI/bookkeeper thing that just happened. Deep down, I think years ago, she thought you'd come after her and tell her that she meant more to you than this company and you didn't do that. She never came out and said that, but she's been my friend since elementary school and I know her. I watched her excitement every time the phone rang, hoping it was you. I watched her get nervous when a flower delivery was made to our job back then hoping they were apology flowers from you. It was hell watching her go through second guessing the decision she made of wanting to be number one in your life and when she didn't see that happening, she ended the relationship. That decision robbed her of years of love and happiness with the one man whom I believe was and is the answer to the question mark her heart is looking for."

Lacey watched him lean back in his chair and waited for her next declaration about her opinion of his and Karen's past relationship.

"Thomas, I know this whole FBI case has hurt you. I know that you feel as if she punched you in the gut. She told me that you even accused her of seeking revenge for the years of loneliness and hurt you caused in her life."

Thomas felt like a knife had been pushed through his heart, reliving the words he's said to her almost earlier in the week. He wanted her to know that he already felt bad about everything he said.

"Lacey, you don't have to do this."

She raised her hand to stop him.

"Let me finish," she said, cutting off his next statement.

"Okay," he said, relenting.

"She loves you Thomas and she always has. It's true that in a perfect world, she should have told you what she was doing working undercover. Maybe she should have even turned down the case because of the conflict of doing her job and her love for you. If she had, things may not have turned out the way they did. She had a hand in going the extra mile to find out who was responsible because from day one, she never, ever thought you were guilty. She called me the day she moved back here to tell me what she was doing and asked my opinion. I'm guilty for telling her to do her job. Not because I'm a big fan of what she does, but I told her she needed to do it, not to find anything incriminating against you, but to find out what was really going on at your company. Her first statement to me about it was that she had no doubt you were innocent. She said the first moment her boss told her about the case, she knew you weren't guilty. She wanted to tell you right away and I had to remind her of the oath she took as an agent. She was in the perfect position to prove to them that you had done nothing wrong and to do that, she had to follow through on her assignment. She had every intention of telling you as soon as Carl was found out, but you found out about her being undercover before she had a chance to tell you. She did all of this because she loves you, not to hurt you. If you think the two of you can't move past this and be together, I think you're wrong. You let her walk away once Thomas, don't let her do it again. Many years were wasted because of stubbornness on both of your parts and I implore you to not do it again. I know you love her. You have to see that she didn't do this to hurt you. She was trying to help."

Lacey was hoping her pleas were getting through to him. When she paused and he didn't attempt to say anything, she thought that her pleas had fallen on deaf ears. She was about to plead a little more when he started to speak.

"Lacey, for starters, I need you to breathe because you've said a mouthful. Now, thank you for coming here today. I see why Karen considers you her best friend and only a best friend would show up and call me a jackass," he said laughing.

"Well, you know a friend does what they need to do."

"When did you fly into town?" he asked.

"This morning, actually. I just couldn't stand another moment of reliving Karen's hurt. She's in

DC miserable because she loves you and she hurt you. I had only planned to be in town for the night, but I'll stay as long as it takes to get you off your behind and on your way to DC to fix things with her."

Thomas laughed out loud. He had forgotten how hardcore Lacey could be.

"Well, let me clear up a few things so that you won't have to do that. For starters, I doubt very seriously if your husband and kids would like you just hanging around Raleigh trying to fix my little life with Karen and leaving them to fend for themselves. Secondly, thank you for being this kind of friend to Karen. Lastly, you don't have to stay another day."

Looking down at his watch, he noted the time.

"So, I've already convinced you or are you saying there is no way you're changing your mind about working things out?" she asked.

"If you had shown up in another two hours, you would have missed me. I'm leaving for DC in a few hours and the only reason I have not left already was because I needed to take care of rumors around my company and handle the staff, getting things back to normal and reassuring them everything with the company was fine and back on track. It's taken me almost a week to get things back to normal, but I did and now it's time to get my woman back," he said cheerfully.

Lacey smiled brightly.

"Well, that's good to hear because my husband told me he was expecting me back tonight."

"I do love her and I have no plans of making the same mistake I made before. When she left me before, I thought a lot about going after her and making her see that we were meant to be together despite my business aspirations. I knew back then that I had enough room in my life for both, but I was younger and hurt that she felt I needed to make a choice. I admit, I did put business first, but I don't plan to make that mistake again. I was angry when I spoke to her in the parking garage. I had just found out that she was working for my company as a bookkeeper under false pretenses. I had just discovered that she was in fact, an FBI agent, assigned to work undercover to trap me in some type of financial scheme. All I could think was that she didn't know me at all if she thought that I would do anything illegal. After a few days, a few drinks and a lot of thinking and harsh words from my own friends, I realized just how hard she worked at trying to find out who was really responsible. If she had not done that, I may have been in jail right now instead of sitting here talking to you and being okay with you calling me a jackass. I was a jackass back then and I was being one recently. Today though, I'm not. Today I'm a man who is madly in love and plans to go to DC and not leave until I convince Karen that we gave up on each other before and we're not going to do it again.

We've spent a lot of wasted years apart and I don't plan to have any more years away from her."

Thomas didn't know what to make of Lacey's next move. She jumped up so fast it surprised him. She came around and gave him a big, tight hug as tears began streaming down her face.

"Thank you, Thomas. Thank you for loving my friend and for realizing you two were meant to be together. I'm not going to keep you any longer."

Lacey wiped her eyes, went back to her chair to grab her purse to leave.

"I'll tell Karen you said hello," he said.

"Good luck with Karen, though I know you won't need it. I already know it will turn out great because I know how much she loves you. I look forward to getting that phone call from her telling me you two have made up. Well, I'm going to visit a few friends while I'm here. I just knew it was going to take me all day to convince you and since it hasn't, I have some free time. Tell Karen I love her."

"I will do that and thanks again. I'm sorry you had to fly out from Texas."

Lacey smiled

"Now that I think about it, I could have called you, but I wasn't sure how much cajoling it would take to convince you. I can get back to my family tomorrow and get back to my life of bliss."

Thomas watched her leave and was happy that things had turned out for the good with his company. Now that his business was done, he had a little more packing to do before making his way to DC where the love of his life was waiting to drop the load of guilt he knew she was walking around with. Now that he was done, he needed to get home, finish packing and go in search of the woman he loved.

18

Karen was trying her best to get back into the swing of things at work. Her last assignment at Thomas' company had drained her. She had just left a meeting where she had been briefed on her next assignment. Her boss, who sympathized with the position her last assignment had put her in, assumed getting her right back into work and on another assignment, was just what she needed. She, however, thought otherwise.

"Karen. Am I interrupting you?"

Her thoughts were interrupted with the appearance of her boss at her office door.

"No, not at all," she acknowledged.

She watched as he stepped in.

"Good. I wanted to again tell you what a great job you did on your last case. I know it took a lot out of you and placed you in an awkward position. It's good to know that you saw the validity behind doing your job and putting your personal feelings on the side for the good outcome you achieved. Sometimes personal relationships become a casualty of this job which is something we have all experienced. I'm sorry for how things have turned out between you and Thomas since I know you had become friends again. At least nothing too person had to be sacrificed. I think Thomas Atwater will be grateful to you that you were able to get the money back that Carl had stolen from his company and people were able to keep their jobs. In the end, it was a winning situation for you and for him."

Karen was hearing her boss, but wasn't listening to anything he had to say. It wasn't a winning situation for everyone. She had hurt the love of her life and he was gone. Though things did turn out positively for him when it came to his company, she had a hand in the hurt he was now experiencing and for that, she would never be able to forgive herself. She understood her commitment to the people she protected when it came to work, but what about her protection? Could there be other cases down the line where she would have to investigate people she considered friends and loved ones? How many of them would she end up hurting in the name of work?

Understanding the commitment she needed to make for her job was clear, but wasn't she entitled to have a personal life as well? Maybe being an agent wasn't for her after all. She had spent many years behind the desk doing her job, but now that she was getting into undercover work, she didn't think she was really cut out for it. Being an agent brought her a great level of satisfaction, but her first case as an undercover agent didn't leave her with as much satisfaction as she thought. She was happy Thomas was exonerated, Carl had been caught and all of the stolen money had been returned. A lot of employees were no longer out of money they had worked years to acquire. Her thoughts had drifted off and she noticed her boss was still talking, explaining to her the casualties of the job.

"So, Karen, take a few days if you need to, because this next assignment will take months of your time and you need to have a clear mind going into this. Remember, no mistakes can be made because a lot is at stake."

"Yes sir. I'm ready and I'm leaving early today to go home to study all of the files for the assignment. I will take you up on the offer to take a few extra days. I'll let Tanya know she can reach me at home if I'm needed before I get back in the office. Is that good?" she asked, ready to get out of the office and get some fresh air.

"That's fine."

Karen watched as he turned to leave.

"Again, good job on that assignment. I knew you were ready when I decided to choose you for it and it wasn't just your past connect to Thomas. I couldn't have done better myself. See you in a few days."

As he left, Karen appreciated his accolades, but

she didn't feel even a little happy about her successful case. She grabbed her things and raced out of the office to get as far away from anything work related as she could. Maybe a few days is what she needed to get her mind back in the game.

**

Thomas woke up early the next morning and looked out of the window of his hotel room at National Harbor, right outside of Washington, DC. He had gotten on the road late the day before and didn't arrive until well into the evening, so he decided to check into his hotel and would go see Karen the next day. He'd already decided to call her to ask if she would meet him for lunch or dinner to talk. First, he would get in his daily five mile run around the Harbor. His morning run always helped him think better. He played over and over in his mind how he would approach the discussion with Karen. First, he would apologize for his harsh words and then move into begging for another chance. Just as he was about to get his run started, his cell phone rang and it was his best friend, Preston, checking in on him.

"Hey Press."

"What's up man? Have you talked to Karen yet?"

"No, I got into town late last night, so I checked in, had dinner and decided to instead pay her a visit today."

"Good because I wanted to wish you luck before you went into the lion's den. She's a great woman and though I don't know her well, I like the fact that she sacrificed her own job to make sure your name was cleared. When are you returning home? I'm planning a pickup game of baseball with some of the fellas this weekend. Should I include you?"

"I'm not sure if I'll be back this week. It depends on how things go with Karen. Either way, don't include me in this one."

"Gotcha. So, how have you decided to handle the situation? What's the plan?" Preston probed.

"I'm not sure yet. I thought I'd start with a big apology with flowers, then I'd go into begging and if that doesn't work, I'm moving into groveling. Whatever it takes to get her to take me back, I'll do it. I lost her once and I'm not doing that again. We once talked about getting married and having kids and my dedication to work curtailed all of that. If I have another chance to have all of that with her, I plan to get it. First, I have to convince her that despite all that has happened, she means everything to me."

"Dude, I hear you. The single women in Raleigh won't like it much that you'll be off the market, but it will be good to see you settle down and finally give my children some playmates before they hit college age," Preston quipped.

Thomas laughed at how Preston already had him married with children.

"I didn't say all that, but I'll let you know how things turn out. I'm about to get my run on, then

I'll give her a call and head into DC. I'll talk to you later."

"Cool," was the last Thomas heard him say before he clicked off.

**

Thomas tried to reach Karen at work, only to be told she was out of the office for a few days. Just his luck, he thought. He didn't know where she lived, so he didn't know how to reach her. The cell phone number he had for her had been disconnected and he assumed it was the one tied to her job. He decided to drag Lacey back into the equation temporarily. He didn't have a number for her either, but he knew that she wasn't scheduled to check out of the hotel in Raleigh until noon and he hoped she was still there. He called the hotel and was glad that the hotel receptionist was able to connect him to her room.

"Hello?"

"Lacey, it's me, Thomas."

"Oh, hey. How are you?"

"Well, I was fine until I got to DC and Karen's not at work for the next few days. I don't have a way of reaching her and I thought you could help me out with that."

Lacey didn't hesitate.

"Get a pen and take this down. Here is her address, home phone and her personal cell number."

Thomas smiled as she rambled it all out.

"Thanks. You are a life saver."

"It's not a problem. Go get your woman!" Lacey declared loudly enough to wake the dead.

"I'm on it, thanks to you!" Thomas exclaimed.

Thomas hung up and started to dial her number then changed his mind. He wanted to talk to her in person and didn't want to give her a chance to say no. He headed to his car, plugged her address into his GPS and headed to her house.

**

Early morning showers always invigorated Karen. As she finished and went in search of the comfort gear she wore when she was lounging around the house, her doorbell rang. She wasn't expecting anyone and had hesitated about answering. She really wasn't up for any company, but when she peeped through her blinds, her heart almost stopped right before it sped up. Standing at her door looking amazing was Thomas. She rushed to open it while her heart raced at seeing him and realizing he was at her door in Washington.

"Thomas? What are you doing here?" she said.

"Hi, Karen. I'm here to see you. May I come in?"

"Yes," she answered and moved to let him enter.

After he was in and the door was locked, she turned to face him.

"How did you find where I lived?" she asked.

"Can I answer that after we talk first? Can we sit?"

Karen led them into her living room. She sat on

her sofa while he took a seat across from her.

She watched as various emotions crossed his face. She didn't know what to think ad wasn't sure if this was going to be a friendly visit or more of what she experienced in the parking garage.

"Karen, I'm sorry."

She wasn't expecting that.

"You're sorry?" she asked.

"Yes, I'm sorry and I need to apologize for what I said to you."

"You don't have to apologize. You had every right to say everything you said."

"No, it wasn't okay and please let me finish."

"Okay," she said softly.

"I'm sorry because although I said some horrible things, I didn't mean them. At the time, I was angry, but that's still no excuse for anything I said. It took me a few days to calm down before I came to grasp that you did what you did to protect me and for that I'm grateful and for that I love you. I really love you and I'm sorry. Please forgive me, *I love you*," he said again, drilling that point into her head.

"I love you too," she said.

Thomas smiled.

"That's good to know because I don't want to be apart from you anymore. Tell me you forgive me and we can finally have the life we dreamed. I want to marry you and give you tons of babies. Help me out of this pain and misery I have been in since all of this ended. I need you, I love you and I want you baby. Don't make me have to live without you again."

Karen didn't think he would be the one apologizing. It should be her pouring her heart out until he forgave her since she was the one in the wrong. He meant more to her, even than her job.

"Thomas, I love you and there is nothing to forgive. I should be asking you to forgive me. You are right. I did all of it because I wanted to protect you and because I had faith in you and in the man I knew you were. I just needed to prove it and I did that. Baby, I was on my way to see you that night when Carl was caught, to tell you all about it, but I wasn't expecting you to show up in the middle of all that. Everything happened so fast that there was no way to fix it then. I hope you can forgive me for my deceit and I do love you. I love you more than anything and finally becoming your wife and the mother of your children has always been what I wanted to be. It may be some years late, but I'll take late over not at all, any day."

"I love you my little FBI agent," Thomas said before standing up and pulling her into his arms, sealing their love with an explosive kiss.

"I don't think I'm going to be an agent anymore. If I'm going to be your wife and have babies, which I want right away of course, then I'll need to find a job that's a lot less stressful and doesn't call for any travel. I'm not sure undercover work is for me anyway. The case took a lot out of me and I don't want to feel that way ever again."

Thomas had a great idea.

"I'll tell you what, if that's how you really feel, then how about you come back to work at the company. We can run Atwater Industries together. Besides, I don't think I'd trust anyone else to keep the company books, but you. What do you say? Do you promise to love, honor, cherish and be my bookkeeper for as long as we both shall live?" he jested.

Without a hint of a doubt, Karen replied, "I do!"

Thomas leaned down and kissed her again.

"What do you say we take this little party to a bed and really seal our love?" he asked.

Karen didn't have to be asked twice as she took his hand and rushed toward the bedroom. They each dropped articles of clothing as they walked and when they reached the bed, they were already naked, Thomas was already hard and her body was already longing to feel him inside of her again. She would be his bookkeeper for life if it meant that their life would be like this forever. As she opened for him, she whispered, "forever".

Join Author Cheryl Barton for her next installment in the Amorous Occupations series with the release of the book three, "The Chef" scheduled for release in mid-October 2013.

The Chef

Chef Charles Watts, owner of "Watt You Say?", the most popular restaurant in Chicago, is looking to expand his restaurant by purchasing the building next door. His one obstacle, is trying to convince his bombshell neighbor, Jennifer Taylor, to move her bakery to another location. Her late-night baking and his late-night cooking lead to some fiery early morning rendezvous.

Go back to the beginning and get your copy of book one of the "Amorous Occupations" series, *The Artist,* now available in paperwork and download.

The Artist

Zora Michaels, a local Boston artist spends all of her time working and focused on her next achievement. The war in Iraq took the life of the one man who loved her and her bohemian, artsy lifestyle. She no longer wants love. She only wants to paint. Micah Prentiss had the perfect life, a beautiful wife, a baby about to come into the world, when that world changed with her sudden passing during child-birth. The only love he ever wanted to experience again was the love he had for his child until the passion he found in a painting reminded him of what true love is all about. Come discover a second chance at love that will last forever!

Other romance novels available by
Author *Cheryl Barton*:

Bachelor Not For Sale

Even self-proclaimed "bachelors for life" meet that one woman that makes them want to slow down and second guess bachelorhood. After suffering through the heartache of what he thought was true love, Duron Knight meets and becomes enchanted with bombshell Taija Charles.

Taija has heard a lot about Duron and all of her body senses are on overdrive when she meets the handsome bachelor face to face. As the sparks fly, Taija plans to show Duron how she can help him mend his broken heart with real love and the right amount of lust.

www.cherylbarton.net

A Designed Affair

In the follow-up to "Bachelor Not For Sale", Loren Knight has been engaging in a secret love affair with her brother Duron's best friend and business partner, Michael Bailey. He is everything she could want and more in a man, but she believes the risk is too great for any type of relationship with him beyond the bedroom door.

Michael Bailey has been fighting his attraction to Loren for years. He has stayed away from her out of respect for his best friend and business partner. Now that he and Loren have finally given into passion that they both have been craving, can Michael convince Loren that what they share is worth the risk?

www.cherylbarton.net

A Perfect Combination

In the third installment following "Bachelor Not For Sale" and "A Designed Affair", Tyrone Davis is the king of one night stands; nicknamed, 'Mr. Love Them and Leave Them'. He learned to perfect it from his two best friends, Duron Knight and Michael Bailey. He never imagined a one night stand would have such a lasting impact, but that's exactly what happened.

Victoria Alston couldn't forget the incredible night she spent with Tyrone Davis, someone connected to one of her best friends. The next day, she disappeared, returning to reality and the fiancé she'd left in Boston while on business travel. They both soon discovered that it wasn't just a one night stand, but a perfect combination for love.

www.cherylbarton.net

About the Author

Cheryl Barton lives in Maryland. In her spare time, she loves reading crime and espionage novels, writing, spending time with her family, traveling, line dancing, karaoke and Maryland steamed crabs. She is the owner of CRBarton Productions, LLC, a multi-media company and the founder of Sisters About Making Moves Worldwide, a non-profit organization focused on spreading love and sisterhood, one sister at a time. She is a member of the Black Writers' Guild of Maryland and the national chapter of Romance Writers of America. You can visit her website and learn more at www.cherylbarton.net.

www.ingramcontent.com/pod-product-compliance
Lightning Source LLC
Chambersburg PA
CBHW031333170626
46807CB00002B/686